"B . . . R . . . A . . . D . . . L . . . E . . . Y . . . ! ! !"
  "Bradley!"
  That's a scream you just heard. Me, I'm doing the
screaming. But since it's in a dream I'm always surprised
when somebody hears. My mother comes running into my
room in her nightgown. She's all excited and upset and she
yells for my father to bring the pills. My mother is very
harassed lately. She doesn't get enough sleep and she
always looks tired. Not only that, she and my father never
go out anywhere, like to the movies or dinner or to parties,
the way they used to do. It's because they're afraid to
leave me alone in the house and I'm too old to have a
babysitter. They think if they stop watching me for one
second I'll run wild and act crazy again. Mostly they're
afraid I'll do something to embarrass them in front of the
neighbors.

PATRICIA WINDSOR has taught modern dance, done free-
lance art, and worked with mentally retarded children.
Now living in London with her two children, she still
considers New York, where she grew up, her real home.
The Summer Before is Mrs. Windsor's first book.

THE LAUREL-LEAF LIBRARY brings together under a single
imprint outstanding works of fiction and nonfiction particularly suitable for young adult readers, both in and out
of the classroom. This series is under the editorship of M.
Jerry Weiss, Distinguished Professor of Communications,
Jersey City State College, Charles F. Reasoner, Professor of
Elementary Education, New York University, and Carolyn
W. Carmichael, Associate Professor, Department of Communication Sciences, Kean College of New Jersey.

THE
SUMMER
BEFORE

Patricia Windsor

To Patience and Ted and Michael and Dorian

Published by
DELL PUBLISHING CO., INC.
1 Dag Hammarskjold Plaza
New York, New York 10017

ISBN: 0-440-98382-7

Reprinted by arrangement with Harper & Row, Publishers, Inc.
Printed in the United States of America
First Laurel printing—September 1974
Second Laurel printing—September 1976
Third Laurel printing—November 1976
Fourth Laurel printing—August 1977
Fifth Laurel printing—July 1978

CONTENTS

Part One

THE WINTER AFTER

ONE

"B . . . R . . . A . . . D . . . L . . . E . . . Y . . ! ! ! !"

"Bradley!"

That's a scream you just heard. Me, I'm doing the screaming. But since it's in a dream I'm always surprised when somebody hears. My mother comes running into my room in her nightgown. She's all excited and upset and she yells for my father to bring the pills. My mother is very harassed lately. She doesn't get enough sleep and she always looks tired. Not only that, she and my father never go out anywhere, like to the movies or dinner or to parties, the way they used to do. It's because they're afraid to leave me alone in the house and I'm too old to have a babysitter. I was a babysitter myself once! They don't trust me anymore. They think if they stop watching me for one second I'll run wild and act crazy again. Mostly they're afraid I'll do something to embarrass them in front of the neighbors.

I don't really blame them for feeling the way they do. I sympathize with them, actually. But I can't guarantee that I will be absolutely one hundred percent sane forever and ever. Nobody can guarantee that. One day, who knows, you wake up and feel very strange. And you find yourself doing things that other people don't understand. That's what Bradley and I did, I guess. Only when we were doing it we thought it was a perfectly normal thing to do. I still don't think it was really crazy and it wasn't as bad as my parents say it was. But I guess it was bad enough. Bad enough to put me in the hospital and make me scream at night and have to take pills all the time and cause my parents all this aggravation. Nobody likes you when you cause them aggravation. It's the number one sin in this world.

Of course, I don't always scream at night. Most of the time I sleep soundly like everybody else. My parents think that when I scream is when I'm having my "problems" again. But I'll tell you that I have my "problems" practically every night. It's the time before I fall asleep that I hate. I lie in my bed and think up all these scary things. It's no use trying to tell myself they're only unreal things I've thought up in my imagination. They seem real when I think them. And it's very frightening, but at least it doesn't disturb my parents who are sitting out in the living room reading magazines and books or watching TV. They never suspect that I'm having all kinds of nutty thoughts back in my bedroom. What I think about is this:

The house is alive. It's a big creature and I live inside of it. Sometimes it likes me being inside and sometimes not. It tries to talk to me and tell me stuff but I can't understand a word it says because we speak two different languages, the house and I. Instead of words I hear gibberish and the gibberish eventually changes into drops of water that run down from the roof like the rain does, spilling across my window in wide sheets of water because my father never got around to fixing the gutter like he said he would. Whenever it rains I think I'm going to drown. I can't see out or anything, all I can see is the water sliding down the window, filling up the world. The house, being alive, can slam doors and open windows all by itself. Naturally, it could also trip me on the hall runners or catch my fingers in the kitchen door. It could possibly lock me up in a closet but it hasn't tried yet. Down in the cellar is where its works are, you know: the guts, heart, gizzard, intestines, all the things you have to have inside you to make you function. In the attic are its brains. I never go up in the attic because I don't want to come across any big fat gray house-brain up there.

Only in the daytime am I safe from the house. Then sometimes I tell myself that the sounds I hear at night are only mice walking around in the walls and stuff like that. But at night it doesn't help to tell myself about mice. At night everything is more frightening than it is in the daytime.

Another thing that bothers me at night is the thought of dying. I don't like to think about it. Once I asked my mother about death and she said it was something that happens to everyone whether they like it or not and since there was nothing I could do about it I should forget about it. Can you imagine forgetting about something as important as your death? Some people only worry about the way they're going to die. They hope to have a painless death, like dying in their sleep without knowing it. My grandmother and my mother always say, "That's the best way to go," when they hear of someone dying in his sleep. They tell each other, "It's a blessing that he didn't suffer." As far as I'm concerned, dying painlessly is secondary to dying in the first place. I don't like the whole idea of it, painless or otherwise. Also, I think I'd rather know when it's coming so I could deal with it somehow, maybe even prevent it. I don't want it sneaking up on me. I used to talk to Bradley about dying. He didn't tell me that there was nothing I could do about it. He discussed the possibility of life after death very seriously. But Bradley. Well. He was different. Bradley could discuss anything. Everything was important enough to discuss with him. He never told you to shut up or go away.

In the old days (that's before I was in the hospital, when I was considered "normal") my parents left me alone in the house when they had to go to a dinner party or to the movies. Naturally, since I was in high school and had been sitting for the Jaffe kids since I was twelve. I never minded being alone when I was baby-sitting but it was different to be alone late at night sitting for yourself in your own house. I mean, when I was sitting for the Jaffes or the Hills or someone I was expected to stay awake and be responsible and it was okay for them to come home and find me watching "The Late Late Show." But at home it was different. My parents got mad if I stayed up too late. They wanted me to go to sleep at the regular time just as if they were at home. I felt scared then but not as bad as now. I didn't know the house was alive then. I just used to keep it inside my head, intact, complete, like a bad tooth in my brain, the whole house and all the doors and windows. I felt if I constantly kept a mental eye on the house the windows and doors would never open and let somebody ugly in.

I don't think I'd want to be left alone in the house now. But, I don't have to worry about that. My parents have no intention of leaving me alone at night. They don't want to risk the possibility of me making a big scene on Ravanna Avenue. They've had just about all the scenes they can stand. So they always stay home to watch their crazy daughter and make sure she doesn't slide off the deep end. But how do they know what goes on inside my head? How do they know I won't possibly die one of their nice painless deaths while they're watching me?

Do you ever know the exact moment when you fall asleep? I hate it. My body goes numb, falls through the mattress, through the floor, down to the cellar where jars and bottles are filled with preserves and pickles and fungus. Falling asleep is like dying. I have to jerk myself back and sit up, take my pulse, turn over and face the wall, turn over again and face the door in case something is going to sneak up on me and tap me on the shoulder. This can go on for hours until I hear my parents getting ready for bed, running the water into the bathroom sink, flushing the toilet, my mother's hair clips falling on the tile floor when she sets her hair. My father gargles with Listerine.

When I wake up the sun is shining, bacon is frying and I wonder when the exact moment was that I stopped hearing my father's gargles and fell asleep. I look out the window and everything is alive and breathing and green and living and near. Except for Bradley.

Bradley was never afraid to fall asleep. He could sleep anywhere, on on a bench in the park, in the library, behind a book in class. It's how he survived. Because he was always too busy to go to sleep at night. He stayed awake all night long playing records and writing poems, novels and short stories. He climbed out his window and went for walks on Ravanna Avenue. The police were always stopping him. They'd yell, "Kid! Hey Kid." And ask him, "What do you think you're up to?" They laughed when Bradley explained that he was just taking a walk. They said he had to go home because nobody in his right mind takes walks down Ravanna Avenue at three in the morning. They bugged him all the time. They would wait for him and slink alongside the curb, sneaking up on him with their silent, blinking blue light. "Hey Kid." Of course they knew his name but they always called him Kid. My mother told my father that Bradley's mother had said her son was "incorrigible" when they met at the Luncheon for The Association for Conservative Planning. But I heard that Bradley's father went down to the police station to complain that it was no crime to take a walk. The police told him his kid should do his walking during regular hours and Bradley's father got red in the face and shouted what on the face of God's earth was a regular hour to take a walk?

Bradley used to ask me to come over and keep him company at night. He wanted me to sneak into his room through the window. I was too scared. I wanted to do it but I never did. I only went to see him in the daytime when I could walk right in through the front door. His mother didn't mind my going to visit him in his bedroom the way my mother objected to me having boys in my room. I guess because Bradley's bedroom was about as unintimate as you can get. You had to dig out a place for yourself to sit down. There were piles of records lying everywhere and stacks of papers and old shoes and sneakers and dirty clothes.

My room is nothing like Bradley's room. My clothes

hang in the closet, neatly on separate hangers. My shoes sit on the floor, segregated into pairs. My underwear and socks are rolled into sausages in all the dresser drawers. My furniture is indifferent to me. It only responds to my mother's touch. It waits for her to come in twice a week to polish and dust with lemon-smelling spray wax. My sheets are taut on the bed and when they are freshly laundered they pin me down like a straitjacket. On my desk I have a blue blotter without any blots. My desk drawers are barren. A few pencils lie in them, unsharpened, old. There is a new package of loose-leaf paper in the third drawer. The cellophane is uncracked.

My only true possession is the copy of the *Ravanna River Times* I keep hidden inside the white prom dress in the back of my closet. I haven't worn that dress since seventh grade, when my mother made me buy it for the class dance because she said it made me look like a debutante. It has been dry-cleaned and put into a zippered plastic bag. Unless she expects me to wear the dress to the supermarket, my newspaper is safe inside its hiding place. I'm not supposed to have a thing like that particular issue of the newspaper. It's what my mother calls dwelling on morbid things. I wouldn't have it if it hadn't been for Jazz Paine. She's been my friend ever since I came home from the hospital. She smuggled the newspaper inside a record album. My mother thought it was very nice of her to come to see me, especially since almost everybody else in Ravanna River was pretending they never heard I existed. I was surprised because Jazz and I had never been friends in school. She handed me the newspaper as soon as we were alone. I put it away because I didn't want to share it with her. I read it after she went home. We played some records and my mother brought in iced tea and cookies and loomed around looking overly grateful.

"Jazz is a lot of fun, isn't she?" my mother asked me later. "I didn't know you and she were such good friends." Neither did I. But beggars can't be choosers, can they? So now I have a friend.

I should explain that I don't go to school. Not for another few months I guess. I'm recuperating and everyone tells me I need lots of time to get better. But the real reason is they don't want me out on the streets running around loose. My mother takes me everywhere in the car. She drove me to the dentist the other day. The dentist seemed nervous to have me in his office. He poked around in my mouth very reluctantly, like he was praying he wouldn't find any cavities so he wouldn't have to invite me back to have them filled. "No cavities!" he announced triumphantly to my mother. He seemed very relieved.

Actually, I'm looking forward to going back to school. Not because I'm so crazy about schoolwork but because it's better than sitting around like some invalid. Also I'm looking forward to seeing what everyone's reaction is going to be. There are going to be a lot of teachers and kids who will be uptight about looking me in the eye. And some who will be cool. Some kids will avoid me because their parents told them not to associate with me anymore. And some will be friendly in spite of what their parents tell them. Anyway, it's boring to be home all the time. My mother nags a lot, especially on the days when she forgets herself and treats me like her daughter from the "old days." She'll get on a kick in the morning and it can last all day. For instance:

"I don't know what I'm going to do with you anymore, you just don't cooperate around here. I mean, I'd like to see a little participation around this house, like your picking up that junk you left out on the porch. Who's supposed to pick it up, I want to know? Do you expect me to run around picking up after you? I can only do so much and no more. I can't be every place every minute. I have a lot to do around this house and at this rate I'll never get it done. Now are you going to go out there and clean up that mess on the porch or are you going to sit there and do nothing? Why can't you put things away when you're through with them? Do you expect me to run around picking up after you?"

Sometimes she'll find something insignificant and pick on that:

"What's your sweater doing on the floor of the closet?" (She doesn't ask me if it fell down accidentally. She doesn't let me tell her it fell down there accidentally.) "Can't you hang it up? Practically a new sweater and you throw it on the floor." (But, Mom, it fell!) "It was no bargain either. I said that sweater was going to shrink and you'd have to wash it by hand every time. I don't have the time to wash a sweater like that by hand. I have enough to do around here. I told you that sweater wasn't practical but you wouldn't listen to me. You never listen to what I tell you. You wanted that sweater and now it sits in the closet. When's the last time you wore that sweater? I don't have money to throw down the drain. I'm sick of spending money on clothes you never wear. I'm telling you it's the last time we buy some hippie thing like that sweater. What do you need a sweater like that for? I wish you'd throw that sweater in the garbage can."

Sometimes I want to put cotton in my ears and take a trip to the moon. But instead I sit there and listen and wait until my mother's voice sort of disappears, and then I only hear the roaring in my ears. That roaring sound reminds me of something I would rather not remember. It makes me feel sick. The hot race of oblivion colliding with my heart. Bradley? Why can't you come back here now?

Why is the future so unceasingly distant from the past?

TWO

On Tuesdays and Fridays at three-thirty I go to see Dr. Kovalik. She wears her hair in a braid that circles the top of her head. She looks very old-fashioned in an interesting way. She isn't young, I can tell by the lines in her face, but her hair is bright red without any gray in it. It's the kind of red that must be real, it's too crazy a color to be dyed. Old-fashioned as she looks, Dr. Kovalik is a lot more with it than my mother is. My mother can look pretty young, especially when she puts on a pair of jeans. She looks much much younger than Dr. Kovalik but on the inside she's got ideas that are even older than my grandmother. Most of my mother's ideas come from the Dark Ages.

I'm afraid to ask Dr. Kovalik exactly how old she is. I never ask her personal questions. I don't even know if she has a husband or children. I walk into her office and say, "Hi. It's me, I'm here again." I always make some inane remark like that when I come in. No matter how hard I try to be witty it always comes out stupid.

She smiles at me. She motions with her hand for me to sit down and make myself comfortable. The way she does it, you know she really wants you to be comfortable; she's not just making an insincere gesture. Adults make a lot of insincere gestures. My parents, for instance, will make a big fuss about inviting someone over and giving them drinks and asking if everything's okay and then they'll sit there with smiles glued on their faces and the moment the person leaves they launch into an attack on how impossible it is to get along with him and how boring he is and how they hope they'll never have to see him again, etc., etc., etc. I don't think Dr. Kovalik is the type of person to do that. At least I hope not.

She waits for me to start talking. Sometimes I just can't think of a single thing to say that's not inane or banal or ridiculous. If the silence gets too obvious, she'll say, "Remember what we were talking about last time, Alexandra? Have you given it any more thought?" Dr. Kovalik is the only person who calls me Alexandra. Everyone else calls me Alex except for my parents who call me Sandy. I think my parents have forgotten my name was ever Alexandra in the first place.

I tell Dr. Kovalik practically everything. The only

thing I don't like to talk to her about is Bradley. Every time I talk about him I get a weird feeling in my throat, as if I'm going to cry. I don't want to cry in front of Kovalik. If I cry, it has to be in private. I keep thinking: What would Kovalik do if I cried? Would she just sit there and wait for me to stop or would she come over and do some horrible mushy thing like put her arm around me? I don't think I could stand it if she hugged me or kissed me. So it's better not to cry and never have to find out. And in order not to cry, it's better never to talk about Bradley.

Aside from that, we discuss everything under the sun. We talk about sex which is something I can never discuss intelligently with my parents. My mother avoids talking about sex at all costs. If she's forced into it she takes a pseudo-horrific stand. Her reaction to X-rated movies is "Oh God." When pressed, she admits to me that perhaps I'll get to deal with sex after I'm married. My mother thinks marriage is the ultimate trip. The end to life. Once you're married, as far as she's concerned, nothing bad can ever happen to you again. Getting married is what you live your whole childhood for. It's the end of the line, the end of the show, and the movie fades out with "The End" across the screen and you and your husband go off into the sunset to live happily ever after. The trouble is, things don't fade out in life. Once I asked my mother if she was happily married and she took a long time to say, "Yes, of course I am, dear."

That "of course" business with her is a dead giveaway. I got the feeling she was gritting her teeth when she answered me. I asked my father the same question. He said, "Sure. Your mother is a wonderful woman, Sandy. I hope you'll grow up to be a lot like her." But I don't think he exactly answered my question either.

More important: Who wants to get married in the first place? Getting married is at the bottom of my list of things to do.

I talk to Kovalik about my parents and their marriage and me. I asked her if my parents might be thinking: "If it wasn't for you, Sandy, we'd be happily married." Or: "It's your fault that we're married in the first place." Kovalik said, "What do *you* think, Alexandra?"

I said I thought my parents were pretty disgusted with me and were trying real hard to pretend they loved me. They probably wanted to say, "We can't stand your guts," but they know it isn't the kind of thing you're supposed to say to your own daughter. Kovalik said she thought there were times when my parents were discouraged but that didn't mean they didn't love me. Furthermore, she said, my parents had their own hopes, dreams and fantasies about what they wanted out of life. And disappointments.

"Being a parent," she said, "doesn't preclude the fact that you can love, hate, laugh, cry, be good and bad. . . . Do you feel a little guilty about being the cause of so much stress in your household?" she asked.

"It's their own fault."

"Whose fault?"

"Their fault," I replied. "My mother's and father's. They bring it on themselves."

"How do they do that, Alexandra?"

"By not leaving me alone, for instance. By always following me around. No wonder my mother is tired all the time."

"They don't trust you?"

"No, they don't! They're always waiting for me to flip out or something. I get so sick of it! I feel like flipping out just to serve them right."

"Would you do that?"

"Sure, why not? It's what they expect to happen."

"And would that solve your problem? Would it make you appear more trustworthy in their eyes?"

"Well, I guess not."

"Then let's talk about how you can work to convince them you are trustworthy. What can you do in order to help them loosen up the controls?"

What I do and say in Kovalik's office is private. She never tells my parents what I say about them. But sometimes the Great Solutions we come up with in the office just don't work at home. When I complain to Kovalik, she says, "We have to work a little harder. Nothing can be accomplished overnight."

Oh yeah?

I'll tell you what can be accomplished in a shorter time than overnight. I can tell you what can be accomplished in a split second. One minute you're alive and the next minute you're DEAD. That's what. But I don't tell this to Kovalik. I don't want to hurt her feelings.

She asks me to bring in my journal for her to read. If I want to, she says.

I keep the journal hidden under the mattress and I take it out on the days that my mother changes the sheets. My mother wouldn't understand it if she read it. But Kovalik always makes comments like "interesting imagery" and "something to work and think about."

I don't always write in it. I forget a lot. Or it's just too much trouble to get it out after I go to bed. Night is the best time for writing in it. Night tells you everything.

Notes from the Journal of a Person Not Quite Sane

October 14th

Tears are like waves. Salty. They get in cuts and burn.

October 15th

Patterns in moonlight climbed but the moon fell. I heard footsteps clattering behind me in the shadows and a ghost crossed my path. Cold rain fell from nowhere. I went walking without myself.

October 16th

Someone is walking around inside of me.

Kovalik smiles and says, "Record everything you can, Alexandra, let everything you possibly can come out."

Hint hint but very subtle. But I never write about Bradley. Not directly at least. Someday, maybe, I'll do what Kovalik suggests: let it all hang out.

But not right now.

THREE

Jazz Paine gives away friendship like old clothes. She's rich, maybe that's why. Nobody else seems to want me for a friend in Ravanna River so I latched on to her by default. I never liked her that much when we were in school. But she takes me out with her and this is a new and beautiful thing.

For the first time since I've been home from the hospital, my mother let me go out alone. That is, alone but chaperoned by Jazz. I guess my mother and Mrs. Paine had a talk so that my mother was sure Jazz could be trusted as a crazy-sitter. She has helped me across the threshold of daily life and I can do what everybody else does without thinking twice. I can:

Walk into Cappy's and buy the Sunday newspapers and bring them home to my parents, thereby making a "contribution" to the family. This is the kind of thing that Kovalik says will reinforce their trust in me.

I have gone into Lark's Bakery and asked for a loaf of rye bread. And Mrs. Lark said, "Nice to see you up and around again," when she handed me the change. And all the way home with the rye bread, warm and sweet-smelling against my chin, I kept thinking would she have said it if I had been alone and not with Jasmine Paine, V.I.P. of Ravanna River? Nobody snubs a friend of the Paines. A crazy person can get by if she has influential friends.

I can present my library card at the library and the librarian doesn't dare to insinuate that I am going to eat the books rather than read them. I can even buy myself a pair of underpants in the shopping mall and nobody makes a nasty remark about it.

But I don't go into Haight & Roth. If Jazz wants to buy some loose-leaf paper or a magazine, I wait outside. I know that in the back where the record department is there will be a lot of the kids from school hanging around, buying records, asking Mr. Roth if he will put one on the turntable so they can hear it. You're not allowed to play a record yourself, but if Mr. Roth is in a good mood he'll play a few bands of something for you. He pretends he doesn't like all the noise, what he calls the "clackaphony," but I think his complaints are only half-hearted. Occasionally he'll put on a classical symphony and tell everybody to listen closely and get a little culture. I used to wish Mr. Roth was my father. But then, you never know how people might act at home with their own families.

Jazz takes me everywhere with her except home. You have to know Mrs. Paine for at least one hundred years before you can get invited to her house. She doesn't particularly like Jazz to bring friends home from school. The only reason Jazz even goes to Ravanna High School is that she told her mother she would flunk every damn subject on purpose if she sent her to a boarding school. Mrs. Paine says there are too many "types" at Ravanna High. She was elected President of the Women's Club for four years running. A fossil in her own time.

But I happen to know from listening to my parents' conversation that Mrs. Paine owes Winterstroke's Grocery Store about five hundred dollars on her charge account and that Mr. Winterstroke suffered an attack of angina pectoris when he dunned Mrs. Paine and she told him to "dry up." He calls her a "mackerel snapper" behind the five-foot-high stacks of Coca-Cola six-packs. That's because she goes to St. Veronica's Catholic Church in Stillwater, while everybody else in town goes to a Protestant church, choice of three. Once I asked Jazz how she liked being a Catholic and she said she only goes to church because her mother makes her.

"What do you do in confession?" I asked her. "Does

the priest make propositions inside that dark closet?"

"God help us," Jazz said. "I'll have to educate you if your parents won't."

Oh well, I know what goes on inside a confessional, I just say things like that to get her going. She always wants to know everything. I figure let her keep thinking she does.

One of the first things Jazz wanted to know when we became friends was whether or not I took the pill.

"What pill?" I asked her.

"Holy shit," she said. "Don't you know anything?"

"Oh, those pills," I said. "No, I don't take them."

"You don't?"

"No. But I'll tell you what pills I do take. I take these orange pills to keep me from getting depressed, and these capsules to go to sleep when I'm agitated and these other white pills to. . . ." But Jazz wasn't listening.

"Do *you* take the pill?" I asked her.

She didn't answer. Instead, she started playing around with my bedspread, braiding the little threads of the fringe together.

"Don't do that," I said. "My mother gets mad when she has to undo all the braids you make. Hey, I asked you, in case you didn't hear, do you take the pill?"

"I heard."

"Well?"

"Well no, I don't."

"Ha, I knew you didn't."

"How did you know?"

"Because you couldn't get them. They don't sell them to minors."

"You don't know much," Jazz said. "You have to get a prescription from a doctor. It has nothing to do with your age."

"Why bother to take the pill if you're a virgin?" I said offhandedly.

"Oh?" Jazz asked, biting the bait. "Who said anything about being a virgin?"

"Nobody said. I was just making a comment."

"Well, if anybody's not a virgin, Alex," she said pointedly, "you certainly can't be."

"Why the hell not?"

"You and Bradley . . . you know. Everybody says . . ."

"Let's just drop me and Bradley," I told her, disappointed that Jazz was just another victim of public opinion. I had expected a little more from her, more originality for one thing. But here she was, like everyone else in town, trying to find out whether or not I had been deflowered.

When I was in the hospital they had a big conference with my parents on whether or not I was a virgin. Since I'd been using Tampax for over two years it was hard for them to be sure, I guess. They asked me a lot of personal questions and they gave me a disgusting examination which the doctor told me was for my own protection. It was very humiliating, all the questions and the prying fingers and I couldn't do a damn thing about any of it since I was half dead, bleeding and sedated to the gills. But what I want to know is: what's so damn important about being a virgin? There I was, having lost practically all my blood, doped up and hurting and they were frantic to know if I had been behaving myself morally. It was like the Most Important Question in their minds. The only person in the world who has not tried to find out about my virgin state in some sneaky way is Kovalik. Oh she wants to find out what's cooking but I don't think virginity is the big issue with her. It's not a way of life to her the way it is to my mother. If I were God I'd make it mandatory that every female is born deflowered.

But for all her faults, Jazz has been a patient crazy-sitter. It's just sometimes she gets to be too much, too involved in the arrangements of life. She sticks people with her assumptions and dares them to deny it. When I'm in bed at night in the dark I think of her, my friend. My Friend. I wonder what she does when she's alone. Maybe she goes into a closet and switches herself off like a mechanical doll. I can't imagine her reading a book quietly or making herself a sandwich or listening to music all alone. It's as if she can only exist when she's with somebody else.

In the afternoon, after school, she comes over and we sit together on the porch, me eating pears and cracking pecans with my teeth, Jazz gulping quinine water with a twist of lemon in it. The storm windows are up, covering the screens, and the room feels steamy. Jazz gossips about everybody in Ravanna River. Every once in a while my mother comes in, henlike, and asks, "Any more soda, girls?"

"I'll have another tonic, Mrs. Appleton," Jazz requests like she's ordering a cocktail. My mother says, "I don't have any more tonic water, Jazz, that was the last of it. Nobody drinks quinine in the wintertime." My mother is very seasonal.

"You know," Jazz says, when we're alone again, "it was a big surprise to everybody when you and Bradley split. My mother, for one, always thought he was a homosexual because he was always going to concerts and buying books of poetry down at Haight & Roth. It certainly surprised her that he took you with him."

She stops talking and looks off into space, her fingers busily picking at the threads in the upholstery of the porch chair. Her face darkens with something angry. Is she angry at herself for being so cruel? Or had she coveted Bradley for her own?

Inside of me I hate Jazz at that moment more than anyone else in the world. But I try to stop the feeling from growing. It doesn't matter what people think about Bradley. He never cared what people thought. He wouldn't want me to care either.

Jazz slobbers her tonic water. Maybe she feels she might have made a mistake bringing the subject of Bradley up. I look out across the lawn and see the sun shining, big and full. The lawn is littered with dead leaves because my father never gets around to raking. Then I realize. By implying that Bradley was a homosexual is just another way for Jazz to try and find out about the two of us, Bradley and me. Another way to find out if I'm a virgin.

Jazz puts a filtertip cigarette into her mouth and lights it. Only she's put it in backwards and she lights the wrong end. The stinking burning stench of the filter smokes up the porch. My mother runs in, "Are you girls burning something?" She looks disapprovingly at Jazz's cigarette.

"I have permission to smoke, Mrs. Appleton," Jazz says politely.

"Just so long as it's out here on the porch," my mother says. A funny smile plays around my mother's lips and she tries not to catch my eye. At that moment I know that my mother and I are laughing at pseudo-sophisticated Jazz Paine who can't even light the right end of her cigarette. "I've got the roast on," my mother mumbles and hurries away. I have a fleeting desire to go to the kitchen and laugh with my mother. Tonight at dinner she'll tell my father about Jazz not knowing which end is up. They'll laugh together. I'll laugh, too, but by then it will seem patronizing. And unfair to Jazz.

"Do you want to know about my mother?" Jazz asks suddenly.

"What?" The sun is going down, slowly. I can smell the roast cooking. I feel liquid, languorous, fluidly at peace.

"My mother. She was sick once," Jazz replies.

"Oh?" Where is the sun going? It's disappearing, leaving shadows behind, letting the night come out from under the leaves, letting the darkness seep across the grass, bringing dreams.

"They tried to keep it quiet but she started fainting in the street all the time. She would go downtown shopping and faint in the stores. Once she cut her head on a supermarket cart in the A & P. They told my father to keep her home because they were afraid of a lawsuit. My father wouldn't have sued anybody because he knew it was all my mother's fault. She was always drinking too much. She'd drink in the morning, you know, have a martini for breakfast, stuff like that. My grandmother told everybody she was going through an early menopause and that it would all disappear in time. But that wasn't true because later on she got pregnant with me and I don't think you can have a baby after menopause. Anyway, when she found out she was pregnant she got so scared she joined AA."

"AA?"

"You know, Alcoholics Anonymous. It's for alcoholics, people who get drunk all the time and can't stop drinking. Once they join, they don't drink anymore. But before she joined she got so bad they sent her to a rest home. A place, you know, like a hospital. The ambulance came and took her away one afternoon. She was screaming mad. She was nuts. My grandmother said it was a shame to do it in broad daylight with everyone watching. She said they should have come in the middle of the night and nobody would have known."

"Did you see it?"

"*Me?* Are you crazy? Of course I didn't see it, I wasn't even born yet. My grandmother told me all about it."

"Oh." It was an inadequate thing to say. But it was all I could say. I wondered how Kovalik feels when people tell her personal things. She knows what to tell them back. I don't. I couldn't think of a thing to say to Jazz about her mother. All I could think of was fancy, sophisticated Mrs. Paine being hauled away in a straitjacket to a drunk's home. I couldn't believe it.

"I told you . . ." Jazz said hesitantly, "because I wanted you to know that you're not the only one who was in a . . . you know . . . place like that. I mean, I didn't want you to . . . I thought maybe you wouldn't feel so lonely."

Then she got up so fast she knocked over her unfinished glass of tonic water and it smashed on the flagstone floor of the porch. But she rushed out the door so fast I don't think she even noticed. She raced across the leafy lawn, her feet scrunching the leaves, kicking up the darkness that was beginning to settle all over everything. My mother came in from the kitchen wiping her hands on her apron. "What happened?"

"Nothing. Jazz forgot she had to get home early."

My mother gave me a peculiar look and bent down to clean up the broken glass. After a little while I got up to help her. My body felt heavy and sleepy.

"You don't look well," my mother said. "Go and lie down, I can do this myself."

"I'm all right, Mom."

"Go lie down," she said, her voice rising. "I can manage myself!"

Floating on the stars at night, the magic goblins falling down. Floating toward my bed, lying on it, rising and falling as if on a wave. I dream about Jazz's mother being carted off in a silver ambulance. Lying beside her, under the same green hospital blanket, is a girl about my age. Closer inspection reveals the girl to be me, Alexandra Appleton, Resident Hyena. We zoom off into the night and the wailing siren wakes up every sleeping soul in Ravanna River.

"Shut up," they all wail back. "Stop that terrible noise."

WHHHHheeeeeeeeeeeeeeclangCLANG we go down the avenue. Down Ravanna Avenue, turn into Main Street, heading straight for the riverrrrrrEEEEeee.

"Stop!" my mother's voice shouts. Then quieter, "Stop please." The ambulance falls into the river and drowns, Mrs. Paine and all.

"Stop screaming, please, Sandy." She hands me a pill and I swallow it and drink some water from a crooked glass. "Go back to sleep now," she says. "Your father will be home soon."

"Good night, Mom."

I sink into the mattress, through the floor, down into the cellar where I meet up with Bradley's ghost.

"Apple," Bradley calls to me, because that's what he always called me.

"Ssshhh," I tell him, "I can't say your name because

they'll come back with more pills and tell me to stop screaming."

"It's okay, Apple, just say it in your mind."

No. Not even in my mind. Things in my mind have a way of getting out when I don't want them to.

Bradley. Bradleybradleebradleeeeeeeeee. The Bradley in my head is alive and real. We dwell together in the river of my brain.

"Good night, Apple," he whispers to me.

FOUR

This time before I see Dr. Kovalik my mother asks to see her privately. I don't like my mother to do things like that. I suspect that even Kovalik doesn't like it but she lets my mother come in "for just a moment, Mrs. Appleton, we don't want to take time away from Alexandra's hour." My mother looks at her and then at me as if she doesn't know who Alexandra is.

"I'll only be a minute, Sandy," she says and she shuts the door behind her.

I try to read the latest copy of *Time* magaziné which is on the table in the waiting room. It doesn't make sense, the words go up and down in front of my eyes. I put it down and look inside my journal instead. I wrote a new entry and I've brought it for Kovalik to read. It says:

> Journal of the Cracked in Mind
> Halloween
>   I am a large shadow of you. I am what you were and what you hoped to be. I am a mirror before you and its reflection after. I am what you are after you were. Without you I would not have been. And now that you are gone, will I grow into myself and become you? We are alike. In vanishing, you have left only yourself behind.

My mother comes out looking sheepish. She tells me to go on in. "I'm going to run over to the store," she says. "Wait for me."

"Sure, Mom," I tell her. Sure, Mom, I won't run out into the street unattended and make a scene.

I tell Dr. Kovalik that I am reading *The Prophet* by Kahlil Gibran.

"What do you think about it so far?" she asks me.

"I like this part," I reply. "Here, I marked it." I read: "When love beckons to you, follow him. Though his ways are hard and steep. And when his wings enfold you, yield to him, though the sword hidden among his pinions may wound you. And when he speaks to you, believe in him, though his voice may shatter your dreams as the north wind lays waste the garden. For even as love crowns you so shall he crucify you."

"And?" Kovalik asks.

"I think it's very religious. I wish it wasn't about God, but about real love between a man and a woman. It sounds like that but I know it's about God."

"Are you sure?"

"What else? It's a shame that everybody is so hung up by a joke."

"What joke?"

"The God joke," I say impatiently. "You know: The Father, Son and Holy Ghost Story."

"By joke, you mean that it was all made up for amusement? All the beliefs people have in God, it's all simply a joke you think?"

"Don't you?"

Kovalik is too smart to answer that one. She waits.

"Well," I continue, "I think it's a joke. It sounds like a joke. If you really think about it, how can anybody believe in all that junk about heaven and hell? It's just a myth, I guess. An old legend that's been passed down through the ages."

"Why do you think such a myth, as you call it, has survived this long?"

"Because people are afraid of dying. So they invented heaven to make them feel safe. It's okay to die if you think you're going to go on living in another place, some fairyland with streets of gold and all that nonsense."

"And what about hell?"

"Well, people made that up to scare themselves into being good. I mean, they couldn't swallow all that stuff about heaven if it wasn't hard to get there. So they made up hell and decided that's where all the bad guys would go. That way, everyone could force you to be good all the time."

"You don't think people would be good if they weren't afraid of hell?"

"They're not good anyway. I told you, I don't believe in either one of them but if it were true, I mean just hypothetically, I think everyone would end up in hell."

"Why?" Kovalik wants to know. I think her favorite word is "why?"

"They're all hypocrites, that's why. Nobody follows any of those basic Christian principles, they just pretend to go along with it."

"Even if it's all a joke, you think people ought to follow the rules?"

"Well if they say they believe in something, they ought to go all the way. I mean, they're supposed to Love Thy Neighbor and all that jazz but I never see anybody loving anyone."

"No?"

"Hardly ever. My parents, for instance. They're always grouching about the neighbors and talking behind people's backs. They got hysterical when they thought some black family might move in on our block. So is that loving your neighbor?"

Kovalik is silent.

"It's all pretense! Nobody loves anyone! Only if you conform to all their stupid rules and regulations. But if you do one thing a little different then they hate you. They really hate you! You can't be yourself at all. If you dress wrong, or if you say something they don't agree with then they get angry, they call you crazy! It's all a lot of junk."

"Does it make you angry that they do things differently than you do? That they believe in things you don't believe in?"

"I don't care what they do! I just want them to leave me alone!"

"Who?"

"Everybody!" I scream. We sit in silence for a while. Kovalik hasn't picked up her pencil yet. Sometimes she writes things down as I talk. But other times she doesn't write at all. I don't know which I like better. I haven't decided whether she writes what's really important or just writes when I'm telling her something boring. But I guess I feel better when she writes. I like to say some worthwhile things and it gets me nervous if she doesn't write anything at all during a session. I go home and look in all my poetry books to try to get some imagery to use the next time. I wish I could read what she writes. Maybe it says something like: "Alexandra is an insufferable bore today," or maybe she's writing her shopping list, "Remember to buy bread at the A & P on the way home tonight." For all I know, she's doing crossword puzzles. I think it's unfair that I never get to see what she writes about me. You tell all your personal thoughts and it's all written down and put into big folders and you can never ever get to see what they say. It seems to me if you expose so many raw parts of yourself you have a right to know what conclusions are being drawn.

"It's all nonsense," I tell her again. "Especially that crap about eternal life. Imagine the overcrowded living conditions up there in heaven!"

"What about hell? Didn't you say that you thought everybody would go there instead of to heaven?"

"You're right. It could be a ghetto. But then if they burn up all the sinners as they come in it would solve the housing problem very well. But eternal life is the biggest joke of all. It's positively sickening."

"It is?"

"Yes! It's disgusting. It's unimaginable. I don't like to think about it."

"Does such a notion frighten you?"

"You bet it does. Eternal life is the spookiest thing going. I always wonder why people want to live forever. It scares the hell out of me. Just going on and on and on. Ugh."

But you really can't go on and on forever. The universe started somehow and it has to end somehow. The end of the universe will have nothing to do with God or Jesus or heaven. It's simply a basic law of physics or something. But when everybody talks so much about life and dying and whatever, it makes you start to think. What if there were something like eternal life? Really? I shiver. I can't stand the thought of it, I really can't.

"I don't know which is worse," I say, "dying or getting eternal life."

Kovalik can't tell me which is worse. Or else she won't. Maybe she knows but I sure don't. If you die you lose yourself completely, you just disappear. So I guess that's why eternal life has to be part of the big joke. Then you're not so scared of dying. I think I like reincarnation better. It can't possibly be as boring as living in heaven. On the other hand, when you're reincarnated you have no memory of past lives and that sort of defeats the purpose. You have to keep being afraid of death over and over again.

Sometimes we talk about my dreams. I only tell her the really weird ones that I can't figure out. There's no sense in wasting time telling Kovalik about a bad dream that I have about not passing a test or something. That's the kind of dream even a dope can figure out. But here's one, for instance, that I bet even Kovalik can't figure:

I am in a big green cage, hanging by my neck. I try to call for help but nothing comes out of my mouth. Down the hill there are some dark trees but nobody's around. The moon is shining. There's a lake behind the trees, I can't see it but I know it's there.

I don't know what a dream like this means but I know it's pretty far out. I feel there's no sense in boring

Kovalik with uninteresting dreams. She must hear lots
of uninteresting dreams from boring people. The trouble
is she never tells me what my dreams mean.

"What do you think it means?" she asks me.

What do I think it means? I think it means:???????
??
A big blank space in my brain. How do I know?
Kovalik is the one with all the answers.

Sometimes I feel it's just a big game she's playing
with me and it doesn't seem fair. It's an intellectual exercise for her to get me to figure out my dreams. On
the other hand, it's always possible that my dreams are
just a little too weird for Kovalik to understand. Maybe
she never heard such weird dreams from any of her
other patients. I guess I can't expect her to admit to
me that she doesn't have any idea what my dreams
mean.

She asks me if I ever have the same dream more
than once. One of the dreams I dream a lot is about
broken windows. I'm always walking on a desolate road,
way up at the end of Ravanna Avenue, or at least what
seems to be the end of Ravanna Avenue. It's almost dark
outside and I'm frightened. Nobody is around. The trees
are blowing, there's a wind way high up in the sky, and
it only shakes the very tops of the trees. It makes a
kind of whistling sound, as if it's trying to tell me something. Then I see the house. It's a big old white house
and all the windows in it are broken. When I see that
house I start to run but my feet feel like lead. I try to
scream and nothing comes out of my mouth. Sometimes my eyes close and when I try to open them to see
where I'm running I can't do it. My eyes get stuck
closed. I have this dream at least three times a month.
But I still don't know what it means.

I do know that the house in the dream reminds me of
the Staneblood house at the end of Ravanna Avenue.
When I was younger I used to think it was haunted. All
the kids used to pretend there were ghosts in that house
and we always went there on Halloween planning to go

inside. But all it took was one look at the place and we ran away.

If a kid wanted to be rotten he'd dare you to go inside the Staneblood house. When you couldn't bring yourself to do it, he'd yell "chicken chicken," but he wouldn't ever want to go inside himself. The few kids who did go inside came out looking green. They swore they heard old Darius Staneblood walking around upstairs and they'd describe how they heard him growling.

Darius Leo Staneblood was arrested for murder when I was about six years old. His trial was the biggest scandal in Exeter County. It kept everybody talking for at least six months. It came out that Darius Leo considered himself a modern-day werewolf. He said he couldn't help doing terrible things when the moon was full. Although he was only tried and convicted for the murder of his housekeeper, he admitted to killing a lot more women over the years. He said he had always tried to get on a plane to fly away from the full moon when he felt the urge coming on. But one day he missed his plane and he went home and killed the housekeeper. He felt sorry because he liked her very much. She was a thirty-six-year-old widow with blonde hair.

Even while Darius was still living in the house, long before his arrest, the house looked haunted. It needed a coat of paint, there were weeds in the front yard and the black wrought-iron fence was broken in a million places. He had lived there his whole life with his mother and father. After they died, he got himself a housekeeper. The thirty-six-year-old widow was the fourth housekeeper he had employed. I don't know what happened to the other three. Maybe Darius killed them too.

They sent Darius away to a prison for the criminally insane. He was there for about five years and then he died.

Of course this all happened when I was six years old and the only reason I know all about it is because Bradley got very interested in the Staneblood family a couple of years ago and he went to the library and took out all the microfilms of the newspaper accounts of the trial.

He was really into Darius Leo Staneblood for about six months and he did his term paper on Darius's obsession with being a werewolf. Mr. Duncan, the English teacher, reluctantly gave Bradley an A even though he said the subject matter was a little "bizarre." Bradley was a genius, he really was.

But the whole subject of the murder frightened me, especially when Bradley insisted I come along on what he called his "field trips" to the Staneblood house. My mother warned me to keep out of that place. She said the floorboards were rotten and we could fall through. I never did go upstairs with Bradley. I stayed in the front hall, shivering and shaking and wishing he'd hurry up and get finished. The murdered housekeeper's name was Alice Avery and I never liked the idea that her initials were the same as mine. When you're standing in a smelly old house all by yourself and you hear footsteps creaking around upstairs and even though you say to yourself, "Those are Bradley's footsteps," you can still get scared stiff.

I remember standing in that hall and silently screaming for Bradley to come back downstairs. I'd hear all the noises the house made, all the moans and groans of rotting wood and sagging doors. The chandelier, hanging high up in the dim moldy ceiling, was the only gentle sound in that dying house. It would chink and chime in the breeze like a surprising touch of light-hearted laughter.

"Do you think that chandelier is worth a lot of money?" I once asked Bradley, wondering why it had been left in the almost empty house.

"No," Bradley said. "It looks like it came out of a Sears Roebuck catalog. Instant middle class."

But to me the chandelier was cut-glass crystal, pure ice, a lyrical laughter in the ancient moldering gloom.

Anyway, I tell Kovalik how I dream about a big house with broken windows but I don't know whose house it is or where it is or anything at all. I don't tell her about its being like the Staneblood house. I don't tell her about Bradley's research into a modern-day

werewolf. Those are my private things. I don't tell
them to anybody.

I let Kovalik keep a few pages from my journal to
read until next time.

Notes from the Underground of the Insane
I promise I will remember the music, and
worship it alone. In death may I run with you to
the last star. Singing, singing. But sometimes I
suspect the music is a demon, seducing me, taking me down, down, with no Orpheus to turn.
How the music confounds me, it kills me, it reminds me of the brisk air of other Octobers.
Someday I will dance on the cold wind, a blue-
bird changing into a crowlike peacock. Turning
turning. But where does the dance end?

I don't think Kovalik understands my journal any
more than she understands my dreams.

FIVE

This morning I felt like writing in my journal. This is
always a bad sign. I should have known it was going
to be a bad day. Writing is such a nighttime thing; if I
have to do it in the morning it means the morning has
caught the night's disease. The sun is contagious, the
air is dark with dreams.

November Journal—Slouching Toward the End
of the World
I heard the sun rising this morning. It went up
into the sky and cracked my heart open. My
blood beat in streaks across the clouds and re-
minded me of wandering on a beach with marble
seaweed. Between the crisscrossed lattices the
emerald light strikes your face in myriad patterns
of green and gold. Don't you hear the elephants

outside? Can you hear them stepping softly as
they go, the casket on their backs, Pavane pour
une Infante défunte. Alexandra Appleton lies in
peace, her face is painted white, her eyes are
closed. She goes.

There's no school today and Jazz comes over.
There's a teachers' conference and it makes the morning feel like a holiday. All of a sudden I think it's going to be all right after all.

We lie around in my room but suddenly it makes
me nervous. Jazz is always doing so many things my
mother doesn't like. For instance, braiding the fringe
on my bedspread and leaning on the wall with her
head. My mother tells me to lean on the headboard of
my bed instead of the wall. She says hair makes an
eventual grease stain no matter how clean you think it
is.

My hair is always clean. It's one of the things I
have a fetish about. I like to wash it almost every day
but I can't do that because my mother says it drains
my scalp of vital oils and besides that it uses up too
much hot water. The hot water is heated with gas and
my father always complains about the gas bills.

I hate dirty hair. It makes me feel dirty all over.
You can't be clean, no matter how much you wash, if
your hair is dirty. I hate it when other people have
dirty hair. Some of the kids in school, they never
bother to wash their hair from one week to the next.
I dig long hair on boys but I can't stand when it's
greasy and dirty. Bradley always washed his hair a
lot. It was pretty long, almost down to his shoulders,
but he always kept it very clean. Even my mother had
to admit that Bradley's long hair was exceptionally
clean.

Jazz's hair is relatively clean. She has dark, curly
hair that sort of hangs all around her face. Of course
there was a period of time when I didn't wash my
hair for at least three weeks. Out of necessity and because I didn't really know what I was doing. I couldn't

even go to the bathroom properly, no less wash my hair. But you'd think they would have done it for me. That's the trouble with a crazy-house. They worry about the wrong things. Probably a shampoo would cure a person in a minute. It's feeling dirty that makes you want to scream and cry.

"Come on," I tell Jazz, unable to bear another minute of her head leaning against the wall, "let's get out of here."

"We're going out, Mom," I call to my mother but before we can get out the door she's on top of us asking, "Where are you two going?"

Even though Jazz is a trusted crazy-sitter, my mother likes to know the exact itinerary. She doesn't believe in "hanging out." She thinks girls should always have a destination in mind because wandering around haphazardly is a sure way to get raped or murdered. I guess she's right in a way except that nothing much ever happens in Ravanna River along those lines. Once there was a hit-and-run accident and an old lady died. Another time a man shot his wife with a shotgun but she lived. The biggest thing that ever happened was the Staneblood murder. We are homicideless, as Bradley used to say. There are a lot of robberies, though. People are always getting burglar alarms put in after their television sets and jewelry have been stolen. Mostly it's like Hometown, U. S. A., in Ravanna River. Sometimes I wish something terrible would happen just to shake everybody out of their complacency. When you live in a town like Ravanna River you can't even imagine or believe that the world is full of garbage. There are all these nice big streets lined with trees and big houses set back in nicely spaced-out lawns. Ravanna Avenue, where I live, is considered part of the "good section" of town. The houses aren't as big as they are on Sugar Hill or Hillside Farms but it's still very, very respectable. For my parents, that's what counts.

Jazz and I told my mother we were going to go to the library and then down by the river for a while.

My mother looked uncertain for a minute, as if she might not let me go out. Jazz said, "And we're going over to my house for lunch."

My mother's face brightened immediately and she sort of sighed, "ohhhhh," trying to hide her delight. "That'll be nice," she said to Jazz. "Have a good time now, girls."

"Why'd you tell her that for?" I asked Jazz as soon as we were out of the house.

"Tell her what for?"

"You know, about going to your house for lunch."

"What do you mean why did I tell her? Can't we go to my house for lunch?"

"That'll be the day."

"Well, we could," Jazz said. "It's just that my mother has these people coming over most of the time and she doesn't like me around."

"And today is one of the days she's having people over, right?"

"Well, there are these people coming from the Ecology Council and it's very important. My mother is very interested in ecology, you know. She organized one of the first recycling drives. She's having this luncheon for them and she sort of would like it if I didn't bring anybody over today but . . ."

"You don't have to explain," I told Jazz. It was getting sickening listening to her excuses.

"I'm not explaining! I'm just telling you. Anybody can have company once in a while."

We walked down Ravanna Avenue toward town in silence for about three minutes. Then Jazz said, "It's true."

"Oh so what. I don't care anyway, let's drop the subject."

Sometimes I think Jazz needs Dr. Kovalik more than I do. I mean, she doesn't realize how neurotic she really is. All that long explanation about her mother is just a cover-up. She fools herself into believing the reason her mother doesn't want us over for lunch is

because of the luncheon. It's amazing that she expects me to swallow all that junk.

We scrunch in the leaves that are still piled up
near the curb. My father says it's a very slow fall, the
leaves just won't stop coming down. The air is still
warm, it's the kind of weather that makes Christmas
and snow seem like a fairy tale.

"My mother gives me a pain in the neck," Jazz says
suddenly. It makes me feel like we're friends again.

We don't bother to go to the library, we go right
down to the river. It's cold, windy, smelling of brack-
ish water. Little waves swish against the rotting docks.

"Look," I tell Jazz, "an imitation sea, a pretense of
alluvion."

Jazz looks down into the water but she doesn't understand what I'm talking about. She stares into the
muck for a long time but it doesn't make any sense to
her. She doesn't know that there are no new waves,
only the ocean crying in sameness. And if tears are
like waves, then waves are also salty tears.

"You must have picked that up from Bradley," she
says and she gets the same look on her face that my
mother gets when I read her my poetry. When I used
to read her my poetry. I don't bother to read it to her
anymore. What's the use of talking to people who can
never understand? Sometimes I think I'm from another planet. I feel like some kind of freak. My parents look at me as if they can't believe their eyes.
Who are you? they seem to be asking, and what the
hell do you think you're doing here?

I have fantasies where a spaceship lands on top of
the roof of our house, and my parents get all excited
and start calling the police and yelling for help. Big,
tall, strange men get out of the ship and come right
into the house and my parents are quivering with
fear and trying to protect me from these monsters. But
right away I know! They've come for me. My rightful
people. My people have come to take me home.
HOME. A place where everyone is like me, where ev-

erybody understands. I get into the ship with them and we take off and leave my parents standing on the lawn, and all the neighbors, everybody in Ravanna River, everybody in the United States watches us disappear into the sky. And I'm happy because I'm going home.

"The ocean's song, Alluvion."

"What did you say?" Jazz asks.

The wind is giving me an earache. I cup my hand over my ear. "Nothing," I tell Jazz, "just some poem I once read."

Jazz wrinkles her nose. She likes to read gothic mystery novels. She must have read at least sixty-three of them and there are still more coming out every day. She buys them at Cappy's in paperback. They all have covers with pictures of castles and loony-looking ladies in long dresses mooning out of the shadows. She gave me a couple to read and as far as I could tell they all had the same exact plot. I told her it was like reading a continuous serial of *Jane Eyre,* but I don't think she appreciated the wit. I think she thought *Jane Eyre* was another gothic mystery writer.

Ravanna River is polluted. Every spring there's a big committee to get the town beach closed because it's a health hazard to swim in the river but every summer it seems like there are kids who go swimming anyway.

I like the smell of the river. It reminds me of something from another life. I really think I must have lived in the sea. The smell stirs an atavistic memory a billion years old, from the time when I was a fish.

"I'm hungry," Jazz announces.

"Well, what should we do? Go back to my house?" It's a sure thing we can't go to her house, what with the ecological council eating her mother's chicken à la king.

"No," Jazz says. "Let's go to the diner."

I start to protest because I only brought a quarter, but Jazz tells me she has plenty of money. So me and old moneybags decide to have lunch in the diner. In order to get there you have to walk about two miles.

The easiest and most direct route is to walk along the highway. Jazz insists we'll get a lift if we walk next to the road. I don't like highways. I have this pathological fear of all that bare pavement, that empty screaming concrete. I can't stand the sound of tires coming closer, I can't stand the smell of the wind from the passing cars. But if I say no she'll ask me why not and then I'll have to explain the whole big fear thing and I really don't want to get into that.

"Let's go to my house," I try suggesting. "We can have tuna fish sandwiches and eat on the porch."

"No," Jazz says. "We're going to the diner. You promised."

We walk across the bridge that goes over the highway and we shimmy down the hill. We have to climb over the chain-link fence to get out onto the roadbed. Actually, it's illegal to walk there and it's against the law to hitch rides. But as soon as we get down next to the road, Jazz sticks out her thumb.

"Come on, let's walk."

"A ride is quicker."

"I want to walk. The walk is good exercise. I need the exercise to build my strength up."

"Oh come on, Alex, a ride is faster. Stop being a chicken."

"I'm not chicken."

"Nobody's going to rape us," Jazz snaps. All the cars, however, go whizzing past as fast as possible. Nobody stops to give us a lift. We slouch along the road, avoiding the stench of carbon monoxide. Jazz puts on her pink-tinted sunglasses.

After about a hundred years, and my stomach falling out every time a car passes, we get to the diner. The diner is near the Jasper Avenue Exit. We walk in between the parked cars and up the steps. My ears are frozen stiff. My nose is red. Inside, it's steaming and too warm. It's early enough to get a booth. Nearer twelve o'clock the place is always crowded. We sit down near the window and the cars race by, soundlessly now, as if we've gone deaf.

"What'll it be, girls?" the waitress asks.

Jazz orders a special, that's a cheeseburger with cole-slaw, tomato, lettuce, french fries and special hot sauce. She wants that plus a chocolate malted. All I want is a plain cheeseburger, no special, no deluxe. I wonder why I feel so spartan all of a sudden.

"And?" the waitress asks. I guess I look blank because she says, "With it? Whatta you want to drink?"

"Oh. Coffee."

"Coffee," she says and then she yells out about the cheeseburgers to somebody inside the pass-thru window.

While we're waiting for our food the boys at the next table start talking to us. They're not from Ravanna High, so we don't recognize any of them. Jazz starts to flirt. She makes comments like, "We're just passing through on our way to Texas," and other equally dumb remarks. There are five of them, and two are stuffing their pockets with the packets of sugar that are out on the table. Then they take the plastic pouches of ketchup and mustard. The next thing I expect to see them go into the men's room to steal the toilet paper. Trying not to be a drip, I try to join the conversation but I get a pain behind my ears.

A cheeseburger appears in front of me, decorated with toothpicks that have cellophane frills. I don't think I feel very hungry until I take a bite and realize I'm ravenous from the long walk. Jazz keeps right on talking with her mouth full. She winks and smiles and moves her shoulders up and down.

"Babybabybabybaby," a voice sings in my ear. Only then do I notice that the jukebox is blaring. I can smell a sharp tobacco-onion smell. One of the boys has sat down next to me. His cheek is right in front of my eye, black stubbled, rubbed raw where he has some pimples.

"Your sister here," he says to Jazz, "she doesn't say much does she?"

"Well she's only a baby sister," Jazz laughs. They all laugh with her.

In the window our reflections are mirrored in the whiplash of the sun. Jazz and I, who don't look alike at all, are reflected as similar dolls, oval heads and white faces devoid of wrinkles and lines and spots. In the world of the window we have perfect skin, innocent eyes, large mouths that smile and display rows and rows of dazzling teeth.

"Here's your coffee," the waitress says to me and plunks down a sloshy cup and saucer.

"Oh thanks," my newly acquired friend says, and he picks up the cup and drinks.

"That's disgusting," I tell him.

Jazz frowns. She stuffs the last bit of her pickle in her mouth and wipes her face with the paper napkin. "Come on," she says to me.

My cheeseburger isn't even eaten yet. Now that I've started it, I want to finish. "Not yet," I tell her. "Wait a minute, will you."

Jazz has left almost all her french fries on her plate. Maybe the boys are making her nervous. She rolls her eyes up to the ceiling and shrugs, taking them all with her in her mocking gesture, making them all of a kind and me alone. Me with my cheeseburger turning to cardboard in my mouth. Suddenly I wish I was home, boring and safe. "Are you finished nowwwwwww?" Jazz asks. Everybody watches me swallow the last mouthful. I wish I could have something to drink but I don't want to drink the coffee.

We have to stop to pay the cashier at the counter. Jazz doles out a couple of crisp green bills from her suede wallet. The cashier smiles. The boys laugh behind us, following us out the door.

"Hey man, look at this, hey comm-mon baby sister, want a ride in my car?" One of them is pulling my arm. I pull it back.

"Have you got a car? Have you got wheeeeeeellllll-ssssssssssss?"

"Oh God, they're going to follow us, Jazz, come on, let's go."

"Don't be so uptight, Alex, they're harmless."

"Let's wait and see which direction they go in and then let's walk the opposite way."

"What? I'm not walking out of my way just because you're afraid," Jazz scolds, her voice is cold.

"How about it, want a ride? Whichever way you're going, we're going that way."

"We're going to Ravanna," Jazz tells them.

"Just exactly, absolutely where we're going. Isn't that right, man? Aren't we going to Ravanna?" They all nod their heads. Five heads nodding and bouncing.

"Jazz, we really shouldn't go with them," I say in my mother's voice. I wonder how my mother's voice has got inside me.

"What's wrong with you?" Jazz asks. "I didn't think *you* were hung up about boys."

"I'm not hung up." I am not hung up about boys. But five of these, sitting inside a blackened metal cocoon. They are not poets, their emotions are sparse, and scrawny and hard. They will take everything out of my brain and put nothing back. They are people who dispose of people, cloggers of the landscape who litter themselves.

"Alex!" Jazz is yelling at me. Perhaps she has been talking to me and I wasn't listening. That used to happen a lot but it hasn't happened in a long time. Feeling scary, like my legs are made of water, I go toward the boys' car. Jazz is already in the car. They are waving their hands as if they are going to take off into the sky any minute and leave me on the ground. Come on. Come onnnnnnn.

I am inside the car now, a creature locked up in a metal cocoon. But unlike the cottony stuff of insects, this cocoon moves across the macadam landscape and turns out onto the highway.

"Which way are we going?" I cry out.

"For God's sake," Jazz says, "we're only going to Ravanna." Everybody laughs.

"Baby sister," the boy who is driving says, "let's fly. Let's go high."

Jazz is laughing in the back seat. She is sitting on

somebody's lap. "Jeff," she says, "quit it, Jeff."

"What's your name?" I ask the boy next to me. I am in the front, stuck between the driver and this other person.

"Huh?" he says. "Oh, Mitchell."

"My name is Alex."

"Oh," he says. That's all we have to say to each other. Neither one of us can think up another thing to say.

We do fly back to Ravanna River, much faster than Jazz and I could ever walk. I hold my breath until we turn at the exit, hoping they won't pass it. The car turns and slows, climbing the exit ramp. Now they'll let us off, I think, wondering why I'm so worried. Nothing terrible is happening. Mitchell is sitting as far away from me as he can get.

But they don't stop, instead they keep driving, through town, past Cappy's corner, up onto Albermarle Street. The houses zip past. We're heading toward the reservoir.

Mitchell leans over and flicks on the radio. His sleeve touches my hand. It's a warm sleeve, it makes me feel warm and easy instead of scaring me. I wish he'd leave it there but he takes it away quickly and looks out the window.

Gotta Get Up, Gotta Go Out, Gotta Get Home in the Morrrnnnninggg. The driver keeps time with his right foot. The car hesitates, lurches forward, hesitates and lurches again.

"For Christ sake, Jonathan!" somebody in the back seat yells. My head tips forward and almost bangs the windshield. Mitchell yanks me back.

"Hey watch it," he says, and his face gets peculiarly red.

"Yeah watch it, Jon," Jeff says.

"Yeah watch it," Jazz repeats. This strikes everybody funny and they all burst out into hysterical laughter. Jonathan swerves and nearly hits a tree.

Gotta Get Up Gotta Go Home Gotta Get Out Out Out. . . . Oh God I'm beginning to feel like I haven't

felt in a long time. I feel like I can't breathe, that my
heart is going to stop that I'm going to die.

"Please, please let us out."

Nobody hears me. They're all singing with the radio. *"Please!"*

I try taking my pulse. Sometimes when I feel my
heart actually beating it makes me feel better. If your
heart is beating blood you can't be dead yet. I can't
help it, I start shaking and then my mouth opens and
I start to cry. "Please let us out now, please." But not
because I'm afraid of them but because it reminds
me. That slant-hilled, winding, sideways pull of the
car, sliding, slipping pavement under wheels, that forest
of black-trunked trees and a fire as beautiful and deadly as the beating of my blood.

"Oh my God," Jazz says. "Oh my God, you better
let us out."

The car stops. It's dead silent. Nobody says anything. Mitchell pushes the handle on the door and the
door swings out. He unfolds himself and stands up and
waits for me to climb past him. Jazz crawls from the
back seat. "Oh my God," she keeps saying as she
brushes back her hair and strokes her clothes to set
them right again.

Mitchell gets back in the car and slams the door.
Nobody is laughing. Their faces look out at me, numb,
disgusted, frightened, awed. "Bad trip," Jeff calls
from the back seat. Mitchell makes the peace sign.

"So long, thanks!" Jazz calls belatedly. "My God! My
God," she says when we're alone.

"It's all right, I feel better now."

"All right! Are you kidding? What got into you?"

"I'm sorry. But I couldn't help it. Anyway, they
were driving recklessly. We might have been killed."

"Oh shit!" Jazz cries. "Oh double shit." She looks
around wildly. "What are we going to do now? Where
are we anyway?"

"I know where we are. Behind the Staneblood
property. If we walk around the reservoir we can find
the path that goes through to Ravanna Avenue. It's

not a very long walk; I used to come up here a lot."

"I'm not walking all the way around any reservoir," Jazz squeaks. "Maybe we'll get a ride."

The wind off the water blows hard and cold and makes my nose run. "I can't stand this," Jazz complains. She has on a lightweight blazer and a red turtleneck sweater.

"Think of something else," I tell her. "Put your mind somewhere where it's warm."

"Oh sure," she says. "The next thing you'll be telling me to recite poetry." Her nose is running. She sniffs surreptitiously behind her sleeve. And she keeps looking over her shoulder as she walks, hoping to see a car. I keep hoping we won't see any cars because I don't think I could take another ride. I keep praying that Mitchell, Jonathan and company won't decide to come back and look for us. Following some of my own advice, I think of other things:

Last fall. It was Indian Summer. Bradley and I went swimming in the woods behind the Staneblood house. He knew where the pond was. Hidden way in the woods, a beautiful, quiet, holy place. It was the most beautiful pond I've ever seen. Everything was so perfectly quiet that we whispered. A hallowed woods. Hallowed ground. Bradley said we better take off all our clothes and swim naked because to wear a swimsuit or underwear would be a desecration of the waters. Trying to hush the splash of our bodies, we swam back and forth until we had to admit that we were freezing to death. Teeth chattering, we ran back and forth to dry off before putting our clothes back on. It wasn't until long afterwards, when I was back home, that I realized that Bradley and I had done something my parents would never believe. We had been together, naked, in the middle of the forest, and it was the most natural thing in the world. They would never believe we could do something like that and not make a big sex scene out of it.

It was a day, so unlike its counterpart, darkness.

The pond was an enchanted place. The earth was my father, my husband, my lover, my brother. Bradley said, "Because we long to dance, birds fly, because we want to soar with them, the winds blow, because we want to be the wind, we are anchored to the ground."

"Stop," a voice is calling. "Stop!"

It's Jazz, shouting at me. I realize I am way ahead of her. "Let's rest," she says. "I want to smoke a cigarette." She gets the cigarette out and fumbles with the book of matches, wasting them in the wind. We sit down on the edge of the road. It makes me feel vulnerable. Every time the wind whines Jazz thinks a car is coming. I don't have the heart to tell her hardly anybody comes by on this road. The wind keeps blowing and my nose keeps running. My ears ache and when I swallow, something deep in my throat throbs. The trees bend like chimneys coming to life. Dark clouds ripple across the sky. "It's going to rain," Jazz says, her voice full of resigned doom. "That's all I need."

"Come on. We're almost at the path. It'll be better than waiting out here."

She won't budge. She deliberately puts out her half-smoked cigarette and lights up another one. "I'm waiting for a ride," she says.

"Oh all right, wait. I'm going." I start down the road again. Pretty soon I hear Jazz come running along behind me.

It takes us at least twenty minutes to reach the path. That's because Jazz keeps stopping because she thinks she hears a car. She looks up and down the road, biting her lips, wishing that a car will appear from nowhere. She might as well be wishing for a flying saucer.

The path was once a logging road. It's overgrown now, the trees and bushes are crowding the sides, trying to reach each other across the long scar of barren earth. As soon as we leave the openness of the macadam road, it seems darker and colder. It's not as cozy as I thought it would be in the woods. I thought I would feel better, more protected, once I was off that road. But instead I feel terrible. First I feel cold and then I feel hot. My sweater starts itching me so much I have to pull it up away from my skin and let the cool air in. Then I get so cold my head feels like it's frozen. I hope I won't get a cold because stupid as Jazz is, I need her to be my crazysitter. If I get sick my mother will blame it on Jazz.

"Are you okay?" Jazz asks me.

"Sure I'm okay. Why shouldn't I be okay?"

"Maybe you should rest for a while." Her voice is motherly.

"I'm fine. Really fine. What's the matter, do you think I'm going to throw a fit or something?"

"No, I don't think you're going to throw a fit or something, but if you want to I couldn't care less." She stomps off ahead of me. Then she stops and turns around. "Listen, I really think you should sit down for a minute. You look funny."

"I'm just cold. That's all. It is cold, you know."

"Then why are you sweating? Your hair is all wet. God, I hope you don't catch pneumonia or something."

"I'm fine. I told you I was fine. Look, if you want to rest, why don't we sit down for a minute. Come on."

Jazz picks up a stick and scratches in the dirt with it. The forest seems peaceful again. I lie down and look up at the trees. It's not windy way down here. The wind is blowing across the tops of the trees, making a soft, faint, sighing sound. It's peaceful.

"How do you know about this path?"

"What?" For a moment I was startled. I didn't expect to hear Jazz's voice. "I used to come up here a lot."

"Oh. With who?"

"People."

"Excuse me for asking."

"You want to know if I came up here with Bradley, don't you?"

"God you're in a vicious mood."

Suddenly I start thinking that maybe Bradley and Jazz came here too. Maybe she went swimming in the pond with him. Suppose?

"Drop dead."

Her eyes jump like a betrayed rabbit. Why did I tell her to drop dead? Part of me wants to say I'm sorry and another part is as dead as lead. It can't move. Inertia, settling all around. I close my eyes and concentrate on not getting sick. Your mind supposedly has power over everything. You can psyche yourself out of being sick. Colds are psychological, they are substitutes for uncried tears. I read about colds being all the stored-up sadness coming out. Alexandra Appleton, I tell myself, I order you, I command you: Do Not Get Sick. But what about sick in the head? How can you get your sick sick mind to make you better?

My mother would have a fit if she knew I had been doing all this walking around. I was supposed to take it easy. I still have a long raised lump of a scar on my stomach where I had an incision in the hospital. It aches when it rains. The trouble with being sick in the head and in the body is that nothing comes out even.

Jazz, feeling angry, jumps up and takes off down the path. She's walking in long strides, mad at me for telling her to drop dead. I get up and straggle along, getting a grump on, enjoying my gripe. The hell with her, I think. But in the next instant I can't see her anymore. "Hey Jazz," I yell, feeling especially grouchy and not in the mood for games. There is no answer. So I thrash along some more, in a hurry to catch up with her so I can blow my top. After all, she is supposed to be my crazy-sitter. She is supposed to deliver me home, safe and sound. The sun is lowering. Everything seems to be stopped and standing still. Even the long baleful sigh of the wind has stopped in the topmost tips of the trees.

All of a sudden, I feel afraid. I have the feeling

that Jazz is there, behind the trees, mocking me. She's watching me and I can't see her and this is the most terrifying thought in the whole world. I want to call her again but I'm afraid of something else, too. Afraid that someone, something, else will hear me. The soul of the forest. A presence that lurks and lingers between the leaves. Pan with cloven hooves. I stop moving. I am all alone. The forest surrounds me. The air is waiting for me to think. It smells like snow crystals. I am the trees. I am the cold grass. My tune is the earth's turning. The dirt is in my bones and the branches are my limbs. Moon of my eyes and wind of my soul. I am so close to time, I may slip through and be home tomorrow, or the next day. I may be home where you are, Bradley. I live within the chasm you left, a burrowed-out place where the only shafts of light are the memories of your words. Oh God, Alexandra, don't get crazy now! Then I hear a walking in the leaves.

"Jazz? Damn it. Where are you?" My voice sounds lame. The sun seems to be falling away at the bottom of the sky. Someone is walking near me. I run. It's just a joke, I tell myself, she's trying to scare you. Behind me. My eyes, straining against sudden dark, see bright, quick images that burn and slide if I try to catch them in my mind. Feet moving on dry leaves. Two pairs of feet. One pair is mine. When I stop, the others stop. Something seems very close, a blacker blackness looming between tree trunks. It's breathing. Help. It's moving and breathing and I am touching the thing with my fingertips. It's totally black now. I can't see anything at all. My eyes are closed. Hard. Soft. Yielding. Warm. Buttons. Too tall to be Jazz Paine. Suddenly I can't breathe anymore. You jerk, you got pneumonia after all. Fingers close over my trembling wrists. "Who is it?" my quavering voice asks, desperately loud in my ears. "You gave me a scare!"

A man. I've never seen him before. Tall, pale, barely discernible. Maybe he's an hallucination that talks and walks. "It's going to rain," he says.

"Who are you? Are you Pan? Will I die?"

"What's that?" he asks. "Come on, you look in a bad way to me."

Somehow we appear on Ravanna Avenue as if we have been spliced into the videotape. Dark clouds are tangled in the sky behind the Staneblood house. One of the shutters is banging against the shingles.

"I don't know what you kids think you're doing," the man mutters.

"I live down there," I manage to tell him. I don't know if he's carrying me or dragging me. My feet have lost all feeling.

"Yeah I know," the man says.

I guess everybody knows me, Alexandra Appleton, resident nut.

My mother's face goes white when she opens the door and sees me. The man explains something to her in Swahili. The long doleful words drag on my mind. My mother gabbles back in an Icelandic tongue. "Gether in sidedon teeperstand yingouww errr."

Pills, thermometers, blankets, pills, hands on my forehead like flying birds. The rain never comes no matter how they moan about it. Instead, snow falls and fills up the dark spaces between the trees. I remember the soft sighing wind in the corner of my heart. I lie in a warm grave and conjure up ways to escape from the monotony of life on planet earth.

SIX

A stiff, dry feeling in my throat. I feel like a leaf, torn out of spring, pushed through summer, now drying and dying in winter's coming. Kovalik's voice seems to talk in my ringing ears: "The hospital is where you got mixed up."

But Kovalik is wrong. She thinks I repressed the hospital and everything that happened. But I can remember it all perfectly. First there was relief. Relief from pain. From bleeding. I was alive. My neck was not broken. My back was not broken. I was not going to be a quadriplegic for the rest of my life. I could move my fingers and toes, wag my tongue, wink my eyes. Aside from the gouges in my guts, I was a whole person, intact, supposedly sane.

But Kovalik's voice is inside my head. Like a built-in mini-doctor, she runs up and down my spine with a stethoscope, pushing nerves, giving orders, saying: Twist this. Move that. Don't pay any attention to that girl upstairs inside the brain, ignore her and do the best you can. The brain, of course, is hopeless.

After a time, I admit, they had to stop treating my torn limbs and my bleeding parts and concentrate on healing my mind. But that doesn't mean I don't remember anything about it.

The hospital was all right in the beginning. It was nice to lie in bed listening to the sounds outside my door. It was like being in a womb where everything repeats itself in an endless cycle of security. Oh, occasionally the other patients played their TV's too loud or their guests made a lot of noise in the corridor, but mostly my life faded in and out the quietness of sleep and meals. The sound of the steam cart woke me up, the smell of food, the banging of metal trays and the clink of dishes. Eat. Sleep. Eat. Sleep. Eat more and have a bedtime rubdown. I drank cool water from a carafe. I went into oblivion and came back in time for breakfast. Faces appeared at my bedside. They smiled, said hello and good-bye. Nobody wanted anything from me because they were all in the interim of being busy-glad that I was alive.

But gladness doesn't last long. Pretty soon they started asking questions. Demanding answers. Whys and wherefores, unanswerable whiches and hows. Forget about the pain, turn away as the knife cuts, remember only that somewhere is a place to go to, somewhere is a home to be in, another country, another planet across the stars.

One day I woke up and saw my mother standing by the bed. She was arranging some new flowers in a vase.

"How is Bradley?"

I asked my mother that simple question in the slatted slidings of sun in the afternoon. I had eaten shrimp for lunch. "Shrimp?" my mother had said. "Shrimp, in a hospital? It must be tough; she can't chew it." The nurse shrugged her shoulders. She said, "Eat up."

"How is Bradley? Is he here? Was he badly hurt? Is he all right? Mother! Tell me. How is Bradley?" Now my mother's face had turned gray.

When you don't know . . . in the silence between asking and getting ready to find out, you can imagine everything. Imagine Bradley falling from a plane, imagine Bradley falling from the railing of the railroad bridge, imagine Bradley falling off the moon.

The afternoon dimmed and went out. A strange brassy edge coating all the furniture. Streets became involved patterns in my mind, scribbles too vague to follow, trees were rememberies on blue slate. Heart beating blood like a numb axe. Sleep encompassed me, and in order to swim to the surface of the languid pool, I had to make a noise. The sound of glass shattering; knocking the glass off the bedside table. It was like hearing the concentric ripples of a pebble thrown into a pool of water. The echoing never stopped.

"What's the matter?" they all wanted to know. "Is something bothering you? Do you have a pain?"

But I stayed mum. I dreamed: Weep for yourself because you are dead. Weep for Alexandra Appleton, gone away and never coming back. Pain that sinks fangs deeper than in reality. Dream pain is the worst of all.

"How is Bradley? Where is Bradley?"

I don't think they ever answered that question.

Kovalik is wrong because I can remember that on Tuesday, August 24th, they moved me to Avalands State Hospital, Hartstein Wing Facility. I can remember the room where we waited with my suitcase next to my foot. I can remember how my foot felt next to the suitcase. I was wearing white sneakers. I kept looking down and wondering why my mother had put white sneakers on my feet. They weren't the ones I usually wore. These were clean, new, blazing white. Dazzling white. As white as sheets, hospital towels, the bucking crackling sting of a straitjacket. "Oh, but they don't do that," I mumbled.

"What?" my mother asked.

"They don't put you in straitjackets anymore, do they?"

A nurse and doctor took me away with them. My mother was crying.

"The reason you don't remember your father being there with you at the hospital is because you subconsciously feel he let you down. You don't want to remember him being there because it would disprove, in a way, the fact that he let you down, at least the fact that you believe he let you down. If he was there, then how could he have let you down?"

Is it Kovalik's voice saying all this to me?

No. I think it's Claudeen Hulle in the group-therapy session in the pink room with the venetian blinds. The sun is always in my eyes in that room. Claudeen won't move over and change her seat; she says I have to learn to face up to life. Do I have to sit with the sun in my eyes to prove I am alive?

Dr. Gianni smiles. He is a thin man with dark brown hair that curls at the back of his neck. He is ephemeral. If you whistle, Dr. Gianni will blow away. Claudeen tells him that she's in love with him. She says he's in love with her but he won't give himself a chance to find out how he really feels because he's got a predisposed opinion that can't be penetrated. Nancy Carlotti snickers. Claudeen says, "Oh Nancy, do you have to turn everything into a dirty joke?" According to Claudeen, Nancy Carlotti is a repressed nymphomaniac who has been made schizophrenic by her Roman-Catholic parental upbringing. Dr. Gianni asks, "If you're so good at diagnosing everyone else's problems, Claudeen, how come you make so little progress solving your own?" Claudeen sticks her tongue out at him.

Nothing makes sense to me in that room. Voices droning on and on, boring Dr. Gianni. Boring me. In the corner a girl with twitchy eyes tells us all to shut up. Claudeen gets angry. Shut-up's echo in the pink sun. The echoes fly out between the slats of the blinds, disappear into the free outside air.

They won't let me go home. They want me to stay. They want to cauterize my soul, give me a whitewashed heart. They ask me to describe the accident. They talk to me about Bradley. They give me pills that make my pee turn green. My mother insists the pills are only Vitamin B. Vitamins will set me free. Chew enough vitamins and I can fly out the window too.

Oh God, I feel so sick, I feel so terrible. I never want to think or talk about anything again. If I wasn't so scared of dying, I'd kill myself.

"Are you feeling better, dear?"

When I open my eyes I'm in my own bedroom. "Yes, I guess so."

"You had a very high fever. I think it's gone down now. You feel cooler. You look a little better." My mother's hand touches my forehead. Her anxious eyes peer into my face. The room is dark. The night light is burning on the wall next to the door.

"I feel better," I say. I guess I do. I feel better to know I'm home, not in the hospital, not in the pink room with Dr. Gianni and Claudeen Hulle.

"Frank . . ." my mother calls out to my father, "Frank! Sandy is feeling better now."

The next morning I have Granola and cream. Granola is my mother's one and only concession to the health-food store. She says everything else is made by unauthorized people. What are their standards? she once asked the lady who owns the store. How do these people know they are doing the right thing? I felt embarrassed but the lady who owns the store was very nice. She tried to explain to my mother that being a big well-known company didn't necessarily make all the canned food in the world safe and clean and decent to eat. She explained to my mother about chemicals. My mother listened with half an ear and a sneer on her face. Later, outside in the car, my mother said, "What does she know about it anyway?"

Why do I hate my mother so much? What did she ever do to me? Try to look at your mother as a person, I tell myself in Kovalik's voice, try to see her as a composite of good and bad, faults and assets. Try not to judge her too harshly.

I feel better after Granola and cream. I feel better after brushing my teeth and having a sponge bath. But something is wrong. Some thick mucus is covering the day. Like a leftover cough, like a dripping nose, it turns my eyesight sour and strange. I feel as if I'm walking through a bad and funny dream.

SEVEN

Today, since I'm feeling much better and it's the last day for a dose of penicillin, my mother is taking me to the Stillwater Mall. Usually she buys everything she can in Ravanna River, saying it's a waste of gas to drive all the way over there. The Stillwater Mall is bigger and better than the shopping area in Ravanna. They also have a Cinema I and Cinema II. I wanted to ask my mother right away what we were going over to Stillwater for but I thought I better play it cool and not say anything. She might have already told me why we were going and I might have forgotten. It upsets her when I forget things. When you're normal and sane and have never been committed to the loony house, you can forget anything you want to and people just get slightly annoyed or they say you had too much to drink or they make any number of excuses and forget things themselves. But if you're a formally crazy person like I am you have to watch your step. Forgetting might be a sign. A symptom that means you're about to go off the deep end again. So instead of asking my mother why we were going over to Stillwater, I just got into the car and looked out the window.

As you probably figured out, I don't feel exactly terrific when I'm riding in a car. But going over the bridge to Stillwater isn't a long drive. I tried to think of good things, tried to push my focus out through the viscid green mucus of the morning. I made a resolution to write in my journal when I got back home. I hadn't written since I had the strep throat.

I tried to think of some kind of conversation to have with my mother. I said, "Did you ever talk to that man again?"

My mother said, "What man?" and jammed on her brakes and scowled at a dark red Volkswagen squareback that pulled out unexpectedly in front of us.

"You know, that guy who brought me home when I got sick."

"Oh, that man you mean. No, I haven't talked to him."

"But you did say thank you, didn't you? It was really nice of him to get me home, wasn't it?"

"Yes." She snaps down her blinker viciously. Is she mad at me for bringing the subject up? All I could find out about him was that he was the caretaker for the Staneblood place. I didn't even know they had a caretaker. My mother said he was probably self-appointed and my father said he thought he was some relative or something. Then both of them speculated on the possibility that the Staneblood house had been left to Owen Andersen. That's his name. He lives in the cottage, not in the house which is a wreck and falling apart. But down in back, past the garage, there's a little cottage that used to be for the summer, or a servant's quarters or something, and Owen Andersen has put in heat and hot water and fixed the roof. My parents think it's a big waste of time because the place will have to be condemned. They also think that Owen Andersen drinks.

"I think I should go over and say thank you myself, don't you?"

"Sandy, I forbid you to go over to see that man! I don't care what he did, nice as it was, you're not to be visiting some squatter by yourself."

Jesus, Mom, I wasn't going to rape him.

"Okay," is what I say aloud. What's the sense of arguing when I know what I'm going to do anyway?

We park in the immense parking lot of the Mall. We get out, lock the car, and head toward the shoe store. My mother says, "Let's see if we can find some shoes to go with that brown suit of yours."

"I think that brown suit is a little too tight on me."

"Oh no," she says, "it's fine. If it's too short, we can let down the hem. I want you to get some wear out of that suit. It cost enough."

"But it's from last year, Mom."

"Oh Sandy, be quiet."

It's warm inside the shoe store. Cozy. But weird, nonetheless. Everything is weird. I try to pretend it's all normal. The shoes I try on fit all right but they feel strange. My feet feel as if they belong to somebody else. Every once in a while I get a scared feeling in the pit of my stomach. I keep trying to relate the feeling to the shoes, wondering why shoes should frighten me. Then I realize it's not the shoes. It's something else trying to get out. We buy a pair of shoes. They aren't bad shoes, but thinking about how they have to go with the brown suit is depressing.

We go out the opposite door from the one we came in. Now we're in the Mall, an enclosed area that's warm in the winter and cool in the summer and has two floors, an escalator and plastic plants in redwood tubs. We have to stop in the five-and-ten so my mother can buy some dress shields for her red wool dress. She doesn't like to sweat. While she's buying the shields I walk over to the candy counter. Everything looks good at first glance. Then a peculiar taste gets in my mouth and everything looks sickening. But maybe that's because I've been taking penicillin for so long. I buy a quarter of a pound of cashew chews for myself.

I guess my mother didn't notice that I left her side right away. Suddenly she comes running up to me, trying to quench the panic on her face. "Oh there you are!" she cries, puffing her breath and trying to be casual.

"I bought some candy," I explain, holding the little white bag out for her to see.

"You'll spoil your dinner," she says, "and don't get chocolate on your clothes." We leave the five-and-ten.

The last stop was the supermarket because it was easier to shop in Stillwater since we were there, rather than stop back at Ravanna's A & P. My mother didn't care much for the Stillwater supermarket. She kept mumbling why in heaven's name they put the salad dressing in the same aisle with the cat-and-dog food. I asked her if I could take a basket and do part of her shopping list. She was going to say no but she stopped herself. Then, very hesitantly, she said yes and handed me half of the list, torn across the center. I did all the stuff on the list and met her at the check-out. It was like I'd been away for a year. When she saw that I had managed to get everything she wanted, and in the right quantities, her face brightened up and she looked like a miracle had happened.

All this time, I didn't know why we bought brown shoes to go with my brown suit. I almost asked a couple of times but I thought the better of it.

Then, when we were back in the car with everything loaded, I got the shock of my life.

"Well," my mother said, "you're all set for school."

"School?" I blurted out.

"Of course," my mother said. "You have to go back sometime."

Maybe I'm dreaming and I can't wake up. But when I sleep it's only shutting my eyes and stepping back into the living again. I want to be burned by the sun. I want the realness to cover me with warm fingers and tell me its name. The one thing I don't want most in the whole world is to wear my brown suit and new brown shoes to school. Nobody wears things like that to school.

My mother switches on the radio. She is giving me glances from the side of her nose but I don't respond. I guess she expects me to be excited about going back to school. But I'm not going to give her the satisfaction. I just sit there, listening to the radio. They are playing "Pictures at an Exhibition." That's ideal crazy music. First strains of it and you are shut out from the world. Shut within yourself and people take on the aspects of cubes. Great white concrete walls hung with magic pictures painted by Picasso. The music is no longer a synthetic pattern of notes and chords and scales but a bunch of words. There is a man in a white suit who walks with a small dog. There are steps going down to a river, the kind I've seen in pictures of Venice.

We zip across the bridge back into Ravanna River. The slush has melted in the streets, there are only dirty clumps of black ice at the corners. But up on Ravanna Avenue the snow is still pure. Our backyard is marked only by birds' feet.

I help my mother unload the car and carry all the bags into the house. My father is already home. He's reading the newspaper at the kitchen table while he waits for the water to boil for a cup of instant coffee.

"You don't want that now, Frank," my mother says. "I'm going to put dinner on the table in half an hour."

"Why don't you lie down, Sandy," my father says. "This is the first time you've been out."

"Go lie down," my mother calls, "and I'll bring your supper on a tray."

Still the same safe invalid, I lie in bed listening to

the sound of dishes and pots and feel safe. If I have to eat my supper prone, then I can't be going back to school that soon. I do want to go back. But first I want to talk to Owen Andersen.

Time to write in my journal. To say things with the coming of darkness:

Still November
  There is a constant quivering inside of me and I have to run and run until I'm somewhere. I want to die if I can get up in the morning and die again. God left and has not been back. I don't think he's planning to return.

Eating dinner is simple. The food slides down and tastes like nothing at all. Then I shut my eyes and feel the floating falling feeling as I try to prevent myself from disappearing in the act of sleep. I can hear my mother talking to my father in the living room. They are discussing me.

"I think she should, Anne," my father says. "She has to start sometime."

"Oh I don't know, Frank," my mother says. "I can't be rational, I guess. I know that I should let her but when it comes time to do the letting, I just back out."

"Well try," my father says. "Make it small at first. Don't push it, just let it happen slowly."

Good, I think in my semi-sleeping death throes. Good good they are arguing about letting go, letting me go, letting me do things all alone, and that means if I ask tomorrow morning to go for a short walk, just a little walk up the street, Mom, then maybe I'll be allowed because Anne will be guilty about Frank and you know you can always get something out of somebody else's guilt. Feeling conniving, slick, sly, supersensitive space girl, I go to sleep with a smile on my face.

The next morning it looks like it's going to snow again. Hurry up, get up, don't waste time because snow means no walking outside after penicillin.

"My you're up early, Sandy." My mother is sitting at the kitchen table with her elbows bent. She is staring down into her coffee cup. Maybe she's meditating on what my father said the night before.

"I feel good this morning, Mom."

"Oh that's nice to hear. I'm so glad." She reaches up and touches my arm, pulls me down to give her a kiss. She smells of coffee and morning and underarm sweat.

"What would you like for breakfast? How about a soft-boiled egg?"

"No thanks, Mom. I'd like some toast and jam."

"But you have to eat something more than toast, Sandy. How about a scrambled egg?"

Okay Mom, I give up, give in because otherwise I won't be able to go to see Owen Andersen, stupid Mom.

"Okay. I'll take scrambled. But not too dry, please."

Smiling, my mother goes to the refrigerator and takes out two eggs, white baby-hatchers gone dead and cold. She cracks them open in a bowl, cracking open chicken wombs and letting the unborn babies slip out into the bowl. Whip, whip, whip, my mother's spatula goes, making a mess of the dead babies. Soon the little fetuses are sizzling in the hot butter, unrecognizable.

"Sandy, sit still, for God's sake."

"I told you I was feeling good this morning."

"Well, don't squirm so much." She gives me a plateful of messy eggs, a piece of toast, a jar of grape jam, a cup of tea with milk and two teaspoons of sugar even though it makes me fat.

"Hey Mom . . ."

"Sandy, please . . . not Hey Mom."

"I'm sorry. Listen. Mom."

"Yes?"

"Listen, can I take a walk this morning?"

"Well Jazz is in school isn't she? Today's not a holiday is it?"

Oh screw Jazz, Mom!

"I thought I could walk up the street a little bit. I

won't go far. I went out yesterday so it's all right to go out today isn't it?"

"Well . . . I don't know. You have Dr. Kovalik at three-thirty."

"But it's only nine o'clock Mom."

"Well."

Oh remember what Frank told you. You have to let me. A little at a time. "Nothing will happen! I'm not a baby."

"I know you're not, dear."

"So can I?"

"I guess so. But just on Ravanna Avenue. I don't want you to get sick all over again. You had a terrible throat, don't forget."

"I'll bundle up good and warm."

"But it looks like it's going to snow," my mother says, regretting her decision already.

"If it snows I'll come right back. If even one little tiny flake of snow comes down I'll be right back. Promise."

"Okay, dear."

But "okay dear" means putting on two sweaters under my coat and winding a scarf around my neck and pulling on mittens and boots and sticking on an old woolen cap that I used to wear ice-skating.

"Mom, it's not Siberia."

"Sandy, do you want to go out for your walk or do you want to stay in and complain?"

"But this hat!"

"Nobody's going to see you."

I look at myself in the hall mirror and I can see why my mother isn't worried about anyone recognizing me. I'm in a disguise, I'm a big walking, talking, overstuffed winter coat with two beady eyes peering out from between the freaky hat and the scarf that's been wound around about sixty times and is choking me to death.

"Okay, okay."

My mother opens the door and looks up and down Ravanna Avenue as if she wants to make sure nobody is out there to see where the zombie is coming from. The coast is clear and she pushes me out. The original Secret in the Attic is sprung.

"Good-bye, Mom," I say, and in order to see her I have to turn my whole body around. I waddle down the front walk and turn around again. Her face is pressed against the living-room picture window. I wave but I can't see if she's waving back. Maybe she's clenching her hands behind her, or holding on to the windowsill to prevent herself from running out in the street without her coat to get me back inside again.

All of a sudden I sort of feel sorry for her. And I feel guilty walking down Ravanna Avenue, acting casual, pretending I have no intention of going back up to the Staneblood house.

Alexandra Appleton, Master Spy. You can't be soft-hearted and be a successful secret agent. I go down toward town and when I'm far enough away from my house so that my mother won't see me, I cross the street and start back up again, hunching over so that I'm hidden by the cars parked along the curb. My boots smack the frozen ground, my hat falls down onto the bridge of my nose, my scarf gets unwound and trips me. I start to laugh. Bradley would love this. Bradley would be jumping up and down behind the cars, a bouncing James Bond, he would be laughing. Sometimes he got so happy he couldn't hold it inside himself.

I'm shivering. Suddenly I wonder what I'm doing anyway. What am I going to say to a complete stranger? Thank you for saving my life. And he'll say, "You're welcome," and that will be it, we'll have nothing left to talk about. Nothing more in common than life and death.

The sun flicks in and out of clouds, the wind moves across the sky. I'm walking in a lonely icecap land, an uninhabited place. What does Owen Andersen look like? I can't put a face on the picture in my mind.

The Staneblood house is at the top of Ravanna Ave-

nue. It's set back in a big square unmowed lawn,
fenced in with a black wrought-iron fence. There's a
gate in the fence with the number curled in iron. But
everything's rusty now and falling apart. Beyond the
house there's a turnaround and Ravanna Avenue ends.
Nothing more but woods, trees, the dark hallowed
forest. The tree trunks all have signs stabbed into
them saying "No Hunting, No Fishing, No Admittance for Any Purpose." No running, dancing, swimming or laughing allowed. Bradley made them his
woods. He made sunlight in the shadows.

But now the trees look like angular bones all done
with life, blind and dumb. The big tree in front of the
Staneblood house cracks its frozen branches against
the shingles of the porch roof. The gnarled trumpet
vine is clinging to the side of the house, pushing its
tendrils in through one of the upstairs windows. The
path leading to the door is overgrown, the flagstones
are split and broken. Weeds and old mud furrows in
the front lawn. I wonder what Owen Andersen care-
takes.

I feel frightened, a feeling in my stomach and
spreading all over. The house looks like the house in
my dream, black windows gaping, and I keep imagining a terrible face looking down on me. I keep my
eyes fastened to the ground, afraid to look up and
see the face.

The cottage is down in the back and I have to walk
around the big porch to get there. Bradley called it
the veranda. The veranda upon which ghosts sat,
asses wrapped in wicker baskets, sipping tea and losing time. That's part of a poem Bradley wrote one
afternoon when he was up here on one of his field
trips. He wrote it on the paper bag he carried a Coke
in. He gave it to me but I think I lost it. You always
lose things when you think you have all the time in
the world to keep them.

The porch is cleaned up now, there are no more
old wicker chairs with pillows hard as rocks and smelling of mildew. Maybe Owen Andersen is cleaning up

after all, the slowest caretaker in creation, he pulls up one weed a day. The Staneblood house looks like a worn-out antebellum mansion. The wind howls.

What if Owen Andersen is Darius Leo Staneblood, modern werewolf, reincarnated? Do werewolves die or do they linger like vampires, sleeping all day? Maybe I'll find him stashed in a coffin, his face like wax, dried blood on his lips. I never did understand how he happened to be there in the woods. No Admittance for Any Purpose. Were his teeth bared, his fangs glinting? Oh, Bradley, I wish you were here!

So what, Bradley's voice says, what can happen? All that can happen is that you die, drop dead, and then you won't know anything anyway. So what.

Bradley? That can't be Bradley. Bradley would never say a thing like that. Bradley never said the kind of things my mother says. I always thought mothers were supposed to help you live. But my mother is very pessimistic. Sometimes after she reads the paper or watches the news on TV she says to my father that she's glad she's not young anymore. Then I look at her and I wonder if being old is in the body or in the mind. Bradley said you got old by looking at too much life. He said sometimes he felt a million years old. But he never wanted to die. He never said So What.

Apple, he'd say, come on, there's nothing to be afraid of. I'll personally massacree any ghost any day, anytime, for you. Apple.

I wonder, is the chandelier still hanging high up in the front hall? Does it chink and chime melodiously in the breeze. But I'm too scared to go inside the house to find out. I don't like the look of the front door. It makes me think of a big mouth. The house is waiting for me to step upon its lips, it's waiting to swallow me whole and alive.

I hurry around the porch to where the path leads down to the cottage. There are muddy footprints in the leftover snow. And little animal paws have crept there too. Some dog stuff piled up. Hahahahahahaha-ha, a voice laughs in my throat. Ha Ha Ha, chilling my flesh, giving me goose pimples, making me swallow hard. The cottage is very near. I'm practically there. I can't turn back now because he might have seen me from the window and he'll think I'm crazy if I just turn around and run.

But I really wish I wasn't here. Why did I come anyway? It seemed like such a good idea when I was home. Now it seems ridiculous.

And then I think it reminds me of something, of ideas in time, of dreaming walking, of sailing flying, of a time and place when an idea grew and grew and exploded.

Do it do it do it, everybody is shouting at me. Kovalik, Bradley, my mother, my father. Ideas not acted on are worse than no ideas at all.

But what am I going to say?

"Hello," I'll have to say when he opens the door. "Hello, I'm Alexandra, the lunatic from down the street, the girl whose life you saved. Remember? It's me," I'll say, "the screwball, the kook, the crackpot, the nut."

It's hard to make my hand ring the bell. The doorbell is new. Inside a lucite cube the name, Owen Andersen, floats on a slip of white paper. Somehow the sight of that new and sophisticated bell is more frightening than anything else. The bell makes me feel stupid and unimportant. He's going to say, "Why have you come? What do you want?" We have nothing in common at all. Nothing in common except life and death.

You said that already, Bradley's voice says in my ear. I know. But somehow it seems very important. I can't imagine why. Neither can I, Bradley says.

I know when I open my mouth only something dumb will come out. But I have to do it.

So what if I act peculiar. So what if he thinks I'm crazy. I'm from another planet. I'm from another world. I don't really belong on earth. If I act weird it's because I'm a stranger in these parts.

You see, I'm not really even human at all.

EIGHT

I don't want to tell Kovalik about Owen Andersen but I don't know why. I tell her other things, how everything seems strange. "I think I'm having a relapse," I tell her.

"Oh," she says, "why?" Her pencil taps the empty white paper on her lap. A relapse is not worthy of mention.

"Everything's strange, it all seems like in a dream. I think I'm stuck in a dream and I can't wake up."

"If you have a relapse, as you say, Alexandra, what do you think will happen?"

I can close my eyes and feel the sheets of the hospital bed under my back. Smell their special smell, dried-out laundry, clean but not fresh. Dr. Gianni's face when he tells me the answer to the question I scream at him. Speak louder, I have to scream again, I can't hear a word you're saying.

"Would you like to be sick again, Alexandra? Is that what you want?" Kovalik asks. Her pencil isn't moving.

"Who knows," I tell her, and look to see if she writes. Alexandra was rude today. Alexandra is a hopeless case, send her back to where she came from, make her a permanent resident of the loony bin.

"What happens when you're sick?" Kovalik asks.

"How do you mean?" I change my position in the chair so she can't see all of my face. I look out the window. There's nothing to see outside Kovalik's window except a gray cement wall and the remains of a scroungy vine that must have been green in the summertime. "Do you mean sick in the head or sick in the body?"

"For now let's say sick in the body. You were just

sick weren't you? What happened at home?"

"I stayed in bed."

"And someone took care of you?"

"Sure, my mother."

"So, when you get sick, someone, like your mother, takes care of you." Kovalik is looking at me but I'm looking out the window. My journal is on the end of her desk. I wish she would open it up now and start reading it instead of looking at me.

"I guess if I want to get sick again it means I want someone to take care of me."

Kovalik laughs. It's a special laugh, gently raining laugh, not hard or cold, not telling you to feel bad or stupid, but telling you that things are happy. "Well, Alexandra," she says, laughing, "congratulations, that wasn't as hard as pulling teeth was it?"

Then I laugh, too. And our laughing together is like something precious, you're afraid for it to go on too long and get tiresome, but you're afraid it will end and then you'll have to look at each other and know that the moment is gone.

"We all need to be taken care of at times," she says, "and our bodies have a way of telling us that we're pushing too hard, just as our minds can get pushed. But there are other times, when we escape from ourselves, or something too painful to face."

Kovalik is asking, Are you escaping, Alexandra? What are you running away from now?

And I think about Owen Andersen opening the door and acting as natural as anything that I should be there. And me going inside with my knees wobbling and sitting in the kitchen while he puts a pot of water on the stove to boil. Looking around for signs of degeneracy, feeling ashamed because there are no liquor bottles in the corners, and when he brings the coffee cups to the table, he smells of cigarettes and smoke. He sits across from me and his hair is brown and lies flat on the top of his head, shaggy in the back, and he has a mustache that droops down on the ends like a sad dog. I can't even remember what we talked about.

He says, when I have to go home, "Listen, you come on over anytime, okay? I'm always around. We'll rap some more soon, hey?"

And on the way home, jubilant because I have survived the ordeal and come and gone, not attacked, not molested as my mother feared. I feel like running and jumping up and down and telling somebody. Telling them what? And then when I get back to my house I have to stop and take my pulse and see if I'm alive or dead because I feel as if my heart is going to stop beating and the whole world is looking at me from the other side of the window glass.

Kovalik is reading my journal. Written in the afternoon with a cramp in my cold hand, because I have the window open and the air is coming in, the verdant, ecru, copper air. Suddenly its smell makes me want to love everything so much it hurts.

> Leaving November and Hurrying to Nowhere
>   Good-bye, piece of me. Words breaking into crystals, exploding into music. I feel myself going with the high wind. And coming back again on song.

She wants to know if I'm saying good-bye to myself. Or to someone else? How can I tell her I feel as if I'm saying good-bye to everyone, this earth, this life. Of all the people who should understand me, Kovalik is the one who understands most. And yet I can't explain anything at all. I realize that the person who comforts you in one way can do nothing for you in so many other ways. And sitting there in her office I feel the way I've always felt forever, alone, an alien, somebody who belongs to nobody.

For some reason, when I get in the car with my mother, I feel furious. My mother pulls the car out of the parking space and her purse falls on the floor and spills.

"Oh Sandy, will you get that?"

I bend over and stuff everything back into the purse and it's like the straw that breaks the camel's back.

"When am I going back to school?" I blurt out.

My mother looks exasperated. She's trying to close her purse and hold it on the seat and drive at the same time. "Well what brought this on?" she asks me.

"Just answer the question, Mom! When am I going back?"

"Sandy!"

"I think I'm entitled to know something," I say, and feel like crying. Damn, who needs crying.

"Of course you are, dear," my mother says, her voice going gentle all of a sudden. "Oh Sandy, of course you're entitled to know."

She puts her hand on my arm and I feel sorry for her. I feel a million years older than my mother. I feel like I'm the mother. "We'll talk to Daddy when he gets home," she says. It's funny that she calls him "Daddy." Usually she says "your father." It's as if she's making me into a baby again. Whenever you show signs of growing up your parents get scared, they want things to change but they can't help being frightened by it. That's why life is such a mess, I guess, nobody knows which end is up. I know then that Kovalik was right. I am saying good-bye to me. I'm not going to have a relapse. I'm going to school.

"Next week," my father says at the dinner table. They look at each other, my parents, and a big sigh of resignation passes between them. They're worrying about how I will behave. I won't ever convince them with words. Maybe for years and years they'll still be waiting for me to go off the deep end. It makes me tired. It's their problem, I think, I can't do anything about it.

In bed, I listen to the house growling. My mother calls, "Frank, where on earth did you put the *TV Guide?*" I feel myself sinking slowly into the mattress and I try not to disappear. A siren blanks out my mind, the sound of the television goes up and down again.

Apple, someone calls to me, Apple, where are you going? Only to watch television, I answer, but somehow the television set grows a mouth, and it opens wide and starts to gobble me up.

I wake up with a big jump, practically out of my bed. My hand is clamped over my mouth. But I don't scream. They're still in the living room, my mother isn't running down the hall to my room. I crawl to the end of the bed and push the window up. The air is still there, tight, scolding, go to sleep now air. I won't ever scream again, I promise myself. And I tell the house. And the house gives up, turns over and goes to sleep at last.

Even though she's no longer needed as a crazy-sitter, I haven't got the heart to tell Jazz. I've grown used to her, like a canker sore in my mouth. Maybe because I feel guilty about not needing her services, I tell her about Owen Andersen. That's a mistake because immediately she wants me to take her up there.

"Why not?" she nags. "He said to come over anytime, didn't he?"

"Oh it's not very interesting anyway," I tell her.

"Oh?" she says, arching her eyebrows. "You certainly seem interested."

People always play the same tunes over and over again. Getting sick of Jazz and her insinuations, getting mad and sorry at her at the same time. And feeling spineless, I put on my coat and scarf and mittens and boots and we trudge up toward the Staneblood place.

Owen Andersen is standing in the snow with a brown dog. The dog and he are the same kind of mind, they stand there and watch us come down the path, not speaking, not barking. I suddenly feel embarrassed because Jazz has on pink eye shadow and it makes her eyes look like they have a cold. Jazz shakes his hand. Owen smiles. Naturally, he asks us to come in.

The first thing Jazz does is inspect the bookcases

and make what she considers intellectual comments about all the authors. I try to give Owen a few meaningful looks but he avoids my eye. He asks her if she wants a beer. A beer! He never asked me if I wanted a beer. I feel like screaming that Jazz is a minor and can't drink beer. The worst thing would be for her to say yes, but she says, "No thank you," in a voice I never heard before.

I walk around the room, feeling depressed. I feel like killing Jazz for being alive.

"Do you like classssicalllmussssssicccccck?" Jazz asks.

"Sure," Owen Andersen says, "that's cool." A smile melts over the corners of his mouth.

I feel like going home. Jazz is thumbing through his records, making comments, and he's listening, nodding, pulling at the ends of his mustache so that they get even droopier.

"Let's play poker," Jazz says. "Do you know how to play poker, Alex?"

"Sure, that's cool," I say but nobody is listening.

"What'll we play for?" Owen asks.

I pull up a creaky chair. Jazz puts her elbows on the table. "Mmmmmm," she says, "well, I don't know . . . uuuhhhh, how about a little game of strip poker?"

Owen looks her in the eye. "Let's make it a penny a point," he said quietly. He turns his head slightly, like a bird turns its eye, and winks at me. The cards make little slaps on the table. The blackened pot boils water on the stove. Owen and Jazz smoke and my eyes tear. Jazz's voice rings in the room, shaking the pots and pans on the walls.

"It's time to go," I whisper to Jazz when Owen gets up to make a second cup of coffee for himself. The dark is coming down fast. All the dream goblins are waiting to get out. I feel nervous. Jazz is smiling, smiling, deaf in the ears.

"Jazz, come on, I have to get home."

"In a moment, Alex," she says, words like sticky syrup.

"Right now."

She mutters, "You're not going to have one of your things are you, Alex?"

"What things?" I ask her, very loud so that Owen can hear. She gets red in the face, caught in the act.

Owen turns. "Alex has to go home now," she says to him as if she's my mother. I expect him to say that's cool but he doesn't say anything.

We put on our coats and hats and mittens and boots, a major production in the small hall. Finally we're outside. Sky dark, smelling of snow again. A racing madness gallops through my heart. Why am I so afraid?

We tramp up the path and behind us, outlined in the lighted doorway, Owen Andersen stands and waves good-bye. I feel panicky, as if it's midnight and I haven't been home since yesterday. I reach up to wind my scarf tighter around my neck. It's not there.

"Oh Jazz, wait!"

"What?"

"Wait a minute, I left my scarf."

She sighs, stops, looks up at the sky. "Thought you were in such a big hurry, Alex."

"Oh wait a minute, if I don't have it my mother will kill me." I turn around and start back. The lighted rectangle of doorway is empty now. The dog is looking out at the bottom, his nose sniffing. My heart is pounding. Then Owen appears again, holding my scarf in his hand. Supposedly people leave things behind because they want to come back again. But what good does it do if you come back too soon?

"Hey you forgot this," he says. He holds it out and for a moment I think he is going to wrap it around my neck for me.

"Thanks," I say and grab it away from him.

"Hey," he says, "do you ever go out?"

The dark woods whisper flashbacks of summer, like quiet footwhispers of birds and mice, sun streaking across a scalded heart. . . . "Out where?" I ask. He laughs. As if I've purposely made a joke. He's waiting for an answer. "Well, yes . . . I guess so. . . . But. . . ."

"Can we go out sometime?"

I feel like my mouth has been hanging open for a hundred years. Think of something to say, I yell at myself. "Well," I mumble, "I was in this automobile accident . . . and I'm recuperating."

"You look recuperated."

I have an overwhelming desire to take my pulse. Something inside of me is pounding, trying to get out. Run . . . run . . . *run!*

"Come onnnnnnn!" Jazz yells.

Walking down Ravanna Avenue, Jazz chatters incessantly. She's crazy about Owen Andersen, she thinks he's fantastic, wonderful, intelligent, she adores older men. I keep thinking about his sad drooping mustache. My mother won't like that mustache.

"Do you think he'll call me up?" she asks.

"Oh sure," I tell her. And I don't know whether it's a wish. Or a tactful lie.

NINE

Sunday morning. I've spent the last three days dreading the phone will ring. But he hasn't called up. I don't know whether to be glad or sad.

This morning we're all going to church together. It's a big event in the house and my parents are rushing around trying to get ready on time. Usually on Sunday morning my parents sleep late or else we have to get ready to go over to my grandmother's house in the afternoon. They spend the whole morning sitting in the kitchen with coffee and newspapers, discussing what to do about my grandmother when she gets too old to take care of herself. My grandmother always cooks something huge like a leg of lamb or a giant roast beef and my mother always has an argument with her about the cost of food and all the extra work. My father always sits in the living room and reads the same newspapers he's already read at home.

But this Sunday morning we're all going to church. Maybe my parents want to pray for my mental health. Tomorrow I'm going back to school.

My mother makes me wear the brown suit with the new brown shoes. I don't have the strength to argue, I'm just glad we're all getting away from the house so if the phone rings nobody will be here to answer it.

By the time we get into the car everybody is feeling miserable. "We're late as it is, Frank," my mother says to my father who is wiping off the back window very slowly and carefully. He gets in the car without saying a word, sticks the cloth in the glove compartment and slams it shut. My mother reaches over and turns on the radio. She knows my father hates the radio on when he's driving.

I sit in the back and listen to the music, hoping he won't turn it off. It plays in the tape recorder of my brain . . . "Sometimes I wonder if I'm ever gonna make it home again . . . it's so far and out of sight . . ."

The morning is cold and the sun is shining. The sky is pure blue without clouds. It's the kind of morning that makes you feel ashamed of your fears. It's the kind of morning that wants to lull you, fool you, make you believe there really are rewards in heaven, that God is up there paying attention. I wonder if my parents are taking me to church to bargain. Here's our daughter, Alexandra, better known as Sandy, please make her sane. Take out all the discord and put in harmony. Better still, take out all that is unusual and make her ordinary. And I'm wondering if I am ever going to make it home sometime . . . somewhere.

The parking lot behind the church is full and we have to drive all the way around and out again and park on a side street. My mother's heels smack the pavement impatiently, clop clop clop, she can't wait until my father has locked the car. "Come on, Sandy, hurry up." My father runs after us, his keys and change jangling in his pockets.

They are already singing the first hymn. The usher hands us our programs, decorated with angels' wings, ephemeral dreams, and we sneak down the aisle to the nearest empty pew. Trying to be unobtrusive, we thumb open our hymnals and search for the right place, open our mouths and pretend to sing. But the song on the radio keeps playing in my head . . . "I won't be happy until I see you alone again . . . till I'm home again and feeling right . . ." Oh I want to go home if I only knew where it is.

The congregation is singing, loud and clear, every believer is getting his inspiration. But I just stand there, feeling like a big monkey, unable to comprehend their joy. And for the first time I feel deprived. Just like the boy in my favorite fairy tale, I've been bewitched by the Snow Queen. I have a big lump of ice in me that's growing and growing and suddenly I wish, I want it to melt.

My mother says, "Oh God, of all Sundays. . . ." And there are Bradley's parents walking in, later than we are. Bradley's mother coming down the aisle in her tweed suit and shiny black shoes and her black purse bumping against her hip as she walks, hands folded in front of her like a nun. Bradley's mother, right next to me, putting out a white-gloved hand that clamps down on my bare, dried-up-skin-covered hand and squeezes.

"Hello, Alex," she whispers, so quietly I think I'm reading her mind. "How are you?"

Hello, Good-bye, Forgive me because I forgive you.

"It's nice to see you here," she says and smiles at me.

And in that smile I see Bradley's blue eyes smiling out of the crinkled corners of his mother's eyes, and I feel like crying crying and never stopping crying.

Amen, the congregation sings. And prays.

Hello, God, are you listening? If I believe in all that business about heaven and hell and life everlasting, will it ever let me see Bradley again? I don't really believe it but I'd like to, for only one reason.

Because Bradley is dead.
And I'm letting go.
Letting go
at last.

Part Two

THE SUMMER BEFORE

ONE

The first thing I do when I wake up is open my eyes and look for the sun. And if it's a sunny day I get one of those anticipant goblin feelings in the pit of my stomach, making me feel like something wonderful and exciting is going to happen. Then I lie there in bed, savoring the feeling of not having to get up right away, watching the sunlight come through the white curtains, listening to the sounds of my father getting ready to go to work. It's summer and I could sleep late, but it seems like I always wake up early when I don't have to. I like to stay in bed and listen to the morning. I can hear my father in the bathroom, the sound of the shower running like rain, the way he taps his razor on the side of the sink. I can smell the toothpaste and Listerine. My mother's voice calls from the kitchen, "Frank, your eggs are ready." And the smell of coffee mixes up with the Listerine. The morning sounds hypnotize me, send me back into a dozing dream where I feel like a little child again. It's so nice to be half awake and know you don't have to get up yet. It's the most luxurious feeling in the world.

I guess I'm a born optimist because nothing unusual ever happens during the day. I mean, nothing that could explain the feeling in my stomach. Alexandra Appleton, optimist personified, always expecting Santa Claus around the corner. I don't even know what could happen. Maybe just life.

Anyway, I finally have to get up and make the bed, trying not to be too sloppy. I'm supposed to make it every morning during the summer. My mother really isn't too strict about those things, sometimes in the winter, when I go to school, she makes. it for me. I'm great at being late in the wintertime. My mother's always yelling, "Sandy, will you look at the clock," and I never have time to fix my hair, so she has to call to me as I rush out the door, "Sandy, will you please get that hair out of your eyes." But in the summer you have all the time in the world. At least for the next week. After that I have to start a part-time job.

After I make the bed I stick on a pair of blue jeans and a shirt and go to the kitchen. Inevitably my mother says, "Sandy, just for once, can't you wear a skirt?" But she doesn't expect me to answer, it's just something she says automatically, I don't even think she knows she's saying it half the time. I get myself a cup of peppermint tea and a muffin. The tea and the wholemeal muffins come from the health-food store. My mother has a special plastic box on the counter for my health-food-store stuff. She's afraid it's going to contaminate the rest of the food.

"Don't forget to pick up that record for Annie," my mother says, giving my muffins the evil eye. "Her birthday's on Friday."

"I'll get it tomorrow, Mom."

"It'll only take a minute to go into Haight's, I don't know why you keep putting it off. You said you wanted to pick it out yourself."

Annie is my second cousin who lives in Stillwater. I'm not really very friendly with her even though she's my age. We don't have much in common. But if I let my mother pick out a birthday present it would be something awful, so I have to buy her a record album or something groovy enough to let Annie know I'm with it. My mother's taste runs to underpants and socks and what she calls practical things and she always says, "Sandy picked that out especially," so it's instant disaster if I don't get something on my own.

"I promise I'll do it tomorrow, Mom."

"What are you doing today? And don't stuff your mouth like that, Sandy."

"I'm going over to Bradley's."

My mother is quiet for a minute. She takes my father's dirty breakfast dishes over to the dishwasher and puts them in the rack. "What are the other girls doing? Why don't you get together with them before you have to start your job?"

"I see them all the time, Mom, they're always at the pool."

"All right," my mother sighs. She thinks a girl should have girl friends. It doesn't make sense to her that Bradley is my best friend. I've known Bradley practically my whole life. When I was a kid, my mother used to make a joke out of calling me a tomboy, and she'd laugh about me and Bradley always riding our bikes together or climbing trees. But lately her attitude is different. She seems worried that Bradley and I spend so much time together. If I'm going to have a friend who's a boy she wants it to be formal. Boys are supposed to pick you up at seven o'clock holding a box of candy and a bunch of flowers and take you out on a date. Then my mother would know what to say, like, "Please bring Sandy home by eleven," and "Have a good time at the dance."

But Bradley just comes over any old time and sits on the porch or we go for a walk or do our homework together. I can't imagine Bradley ringing the doorbell with a box of candy and a bunch of flowers. Bradley is just Bradley.

"How about some cereal?" my mother asks when I get up from the table with my dishes.

"No thanks, Mom, I have to go."

And I give her a kiss on the cheek and start to run out the door, the goblin still inside me, teasing me with inexplicable excitement.

My mother calls, "Sandy! Your vitamin," and I run back and grab the vitamin and go out again, chomping it between my teeth. Outside, the world is beautiful.

To get to Bradley's house I have to walk down Ravanna Avenue and cut into Oak Street. Bradley lives one block over on Kenworth Avenue. It's not very far. Oak Street is short and has no sidewalks and there are weeds and flowers growing next to the road, and for some reason I feel like touching everything, holding the flowers, smelling the weeds, stroking the sticky stems, tasting the sunlight. My heart feels full of something good. I'm glad it's summer, I'm glad it's just the beginning of everything that might happen. The only problem is the horrible taste of vitamin in my mouth. Surreptitiously, I try to spit it out.

Bradley's house is the third one down. On his front step is a redwood tub of petunias and geraniums. In between the leaves, his neighbor's cat is sleeping, bending all the leaves and buds. Bradley's mother doesn't like cats, she's always chasing this one. It's gray with white paws. But Bradley lets it come into his room through his window at night. Sometimes I think Bradley would like to invite the whole world to come in through his window.

I go around to the kitchen door because that's where Bradley's mother always is in the morning. She does what my mother does after her husband has gone to the office, she sits at the kitchen table and drinks a cup of coffee and reads the newspaper. Only Bradley's mother looks glamorous in her long deep blue silky robe. My mother never looks elegant in the morning. Maybe because I'm not a boy.

"Hi," I say through the screen door. I can see her sitting there in her blue robe.

"Good morning, Alex," she says, and comes to unhook the door. She always has the screen door hooked because once the plumber walked right in and went upstairs when she was taking a shower. My mother probably would have fainted but Bradley's mother said, "Excuse me, would you mind waiting downstairs until I'm through?" I think the plumber almost fainted. Bradley says it's his mother's favorite story and she always tells it at cocktail parties. Bradley thinks his mother is a little boring but he always teases her in a way that makes me know he likes her.

"Bradley's in the usual," she says, holding her coffee cup in one hand and a cigarette in the other. She uses a cigarette holder to siphon out the tars. It makes her look like a movie star. "Tell him not to forget the wash," she says. "He promised to dig it out this morning." She coughs a deep growling cough. I don't think her cigarette holder is saving her from anything.

I like Bradley's parents. I once told him I liked them a lot better than my own. Bradley said not to be misled by appearances, that his parents were about as good or bad as any parents are. "But I guess," he said, "familiarity breeds contempt." He said it in his imitation Mr. Duncan voice. Mr. Duncan always uses hackneyed expressions to illustrate a point even though he's the English teacher and is always telling us to be original.

"Listen to this," Bradley says when I walk into his room. He's lying on the floor, his head propped up by books. He's wearing a pair of cut-off Levi's and the dirtiest shirt you can imagine. He reads from a typewritten page, "George White was a nightcatcher in the Charon Division. He wore an acid green jumpsuit with the EE insignia of the Ecology Engineers. Beneath the insignia his classification badge was pinned, a gold sailboat with a red star. George was Double Zero with an ET possibility. When he reached the age of one hundred and fifty years he had a chance to play the computer for eternal life. If he was lucky, he could live forever. George was only twenty-five. He had a long way to go."

"That's great," I tell him, "but what does it mean?"

"Didn't I read you this yet?" he asks, startled, and leans up on one elbow. "This is the science-fiction book I've been working on. It's about life where nobody dies, a disease of undeath caused by the side effects of a cancer-curing drug. With it, all the cancer in the world is cured but the trouble is that nobody ever dies. In order to eliminate the serious population explosion, the government gives out classifications to all babies when they are born. Double Zero is the highest, it means you get a chance to live forever.

Wait a minute . . ." He gets up and scrounges in a stack of papers under his desk. "Here's another character, Harry Ingram. He's running for President of the United States. His platform is Natural Death. He wants people to have secret codes so they won't know exactly when they're going to die. You see, the way it works now, everyone can read his own classification number. Everyone knows precisely the year, day and hour of his death." Bradley stops reading and looks at me. "It's a terrible strain on the nervous system."

He laughs, his own Bradley laugh, a sound that follows me like music. "Your mother said to dig out the wash," I tell him when he sobers up.

"Oh yeah," he says and looks around, abstracted. You can bet Bradley doesn't even know what laundry is, no less find it in his room.

I love Bradley's room. It radiates brains, love, happiness, Bradley. It's the biggest mess in the world. He finds a pillowcase and starts looking around under the bed and in the corners. He starts stuffing the case with anything, old socks, dirty undershirts, old sneakers.

"Hey let's go down to the river," he says. "Maybe we can get Taylor's boat."

"Yeah let's go down to the river and get Taylor's boat," I say.

"Isn't that a good idea?" he asks, doubtful.

"It better be since Taylor is waiting for us with his boat."

Bradley laughing at himself is the most beautiful thing in the world. His mother calls out, "Bradley, will you please keep it down?" We have to cover our mouths to stifle the noise.

"I think I better change my shirt," he says. He pulls a relatively clean one out of an overflowing drawer. He takes off the dirty one, throws it on the floor, sticks on the clean one. "Okay," he says, "let's go."

"Don't forget the laundry," I have to remind him. He picks it up, grabs my hand, we go flying out of his

room, drop the laundry in the kitchen, unhook the
screen door and let it bang behind us. Then we're running through the grass, down the street.

Life clutching my heart so tightly, a thousand years
in a moment, the sun like a drum beating time to
Bradley's footsteps, making everything happen, making me glad.

On the way to the river, taking the shortcut to South
Street, Bradley whistles "Pictures at an Exhibition."
He calls it his walking-on-the-water music. Water
makes Bradley philosophical. Did I tell you he was a
genius? I know it sounds corny but Bradley is one of
those people who can tell you things you never thought
you could imagine. A lot of the kids in school don't
understand Bradley. They think he's some kind of
mental case because he reads things like metaphys-
ics and Spinoza. He reads everything and it all stays
in his brain, being sifted, nurtured, digested, punched
into the Bradley computer ready to come out any old
time.

Taylor has his boat at the old dock on South Street.
Taylor is tall and stringy and very quiet. He never calls
Bradley a nut. They have this sort of silent relation-
ship with Bradley doing all the thinking and Taylor
saying nothing. The boat is just a rowboat, painted
red, white and blue. On the end it says TNT which
happens to be Taylor's real initials.

He's waiting, his feet hanging over the end of the
dock, the boat sloshing beside him. "You got a nice
day," Taylor says, squinting across the river, looking
very nautical.

"Are you coming?" Bradley asks. The boat squeaks
against the dock, the oars bump in the locks.

"Work, man." He watches us shove off. "Don't
rack up," he yells. Taylor waves us down the river.
Like we were sailing to the end of the world. The water is dead calm and smells like old feet. An empty
potato-chip bag floats by. I close my eyes against the
sun, tip back my head, see red and purple fire on my

eyelids. All the noise of Ravanna River traffic fades away, I hear only the sound of the oars dipping in and out of the water.

"Polluted but peaceful," Bradley says. "Let's go to Sugar Creek."

At the end of the town, where the bridge goes across to Stillwater, the river forks and sort of spreads itself out into a swampy area that smells terrible. Beyond that is Sugar Creek, a muddy, skinny tributary winding its way below Sugar Hill. I guess once all the big houses on Sugar Hill had docks and boats tied up in the creek. But nobody bothers anymore. They haven't got the time or inclination to look and see how dirty the creek is getting. And they probably don't want to think about what might be running down the hill to join those waters. So they let the docks get rotten and the bank get overgrown, and only once in a while when some kids have a beer party down there do they make a few comments like, "We have to get Sugar Creek cleaned up," or "Those old docks are dangerous, somebody is going to get hurt."

They say things like that about once a year at the Association for Conservative Planning. Bradley's and my mother belong to it. They see each other at the meetings and they talk to each other there, but that's about all the communication between them. Sometimes I think they're jealous of each other because Bradley and I are friends. My mother never says she doesn't like Bradley's mother but if ever she has to call up because I'm late she gets mad. I never know which thing makes my mother angrier, the fact that I'm late for dinner or the fact that she had to make a phone call and talk to Bradley's mother.

"Apple," Bradley says, "wake up." I open my eyes and see Bradley standing in the water up to his knees. We have to pull the boat through part of the swamp where it's too shallow. My feet squinch in the slime, I hate the feeling. We squish and gush our way to the creek, and when we get back in the boat our legs are muddy brown and we start getting bitten by about ten thousand flies.

But then in the creek, under the trees, the sun is gone, the flies are gone, the green pours down and shades our souls so that we can think we are Indians, ghosts, people from another world, the last two people on a planet where only good things are alive.

I almost say, "We forgot to bring lunch." But looking at Bradley's face, I have to bite my tongue. How can I be so practical when all we need is this moving silence surrounding us. I feel as if we will go on forever, Bradley and I, in an endless summer sailing through muted green lights and shadows, never speaking but talking with our minds. He smiles at me. Blue eyes like sea water. White teeth in a face that seems so familiar and yet suddenly so strange.

I look at Bradley and I know that he and the antici-pant goblin inside of me are one.

TWO

Why do people always think of things to say after the moment to say them has gone? It happens to my parents all the time. They'll have some kind of argument with someone and afterwards they keep complaining about how they should have said this or they should have said that. I guess I never really understood how your mind can get tongue-tied until right now. So here I am, writing a journal in the dark, using a flashlight under the sheets because my mother has already come in twice to tell me to put out the light and go to sleep. I'm writing down all the things I wish I'd said to Bradley this afternoon.

I wonder if all journals and diaries begin with something profound. Or do diary keepers just decide they want a running record of the weather, the world situation and what they ate for breakfast? I never thought

about bothering with a journal before. But all through
dinner and the rest of the evening I kept sliding on
my mind back to Sugar Creek, imagining myself talking to Bradley, telling him everything I had neglected
to say. "What's the matter, Sandy?" my mother wanted
to know at the dinner table. How could I explain to
her that I wasn't at the table at all?

It seemed like such a waste, to have all these un-
spoken thoughts in my head. I knew I had to have a
place to put them down. So I found the small black
loose-leaf notebook I used to use for Sunday school
and I pulled out all the old Sunday-school notes and
started to write a journal.

I wrote:

> In the Trees, July's Beginning
> Here, take this soaring soul of me. Take my
> hand, for in your hand mine becomes beautiful.
> Bless you for walking so near me, your stepping is
> like soft footwhispers of doves and angels. You
> are the sun, streaking across the scalded beach.
> Now I am awake. I am no longer a shapeless
> perambulate in the mist. I have become you. Part,
> and counterpart.

I read what I have written and it seems so inadequate. How can you put the beatings of your heart
into words on paper? I wish I was a composer so I
could write a symphony. Then I tell myself, Alexandra, you are not only an optimistic nut but you are
also an incurable romantic. And I feel happy and sad
at the same time, bittersweet sad because I think I
may be wrong. Maybe what I think has happened has
not happened at all.

And I have to go over it all again. The moments
stretch themselves out like elongated crystal drops of
clear rain. And the rain beats not only in my mind but
on the roof, drowning out the sounds of the world.

I click off the flashlight and stick the notebook un-

der my pillow. Then I lie there, the rain making a
cocoon of loneliness so I can think.

I think of Bradley. And me. Covered with mud, hot
and sticky from working our way up Sugar Creek. We
stop under the big willow tree and put our feet into the
water. The heat melts down the tops of our bodies but
the water is cool. We sit there, half hot, half cold,
dangling words into the water and kicking our toes.
Then we both have the same idea at the same time.
"Come on, let's go in."

Without deciding, without speaking, we repeat a
ritual from an Indian-summer day last year. We take
off our clothes and let our naked bodies slip into the
water. A hallowed time in a hallowed pond. Our
nakedness had never touched.

And I become aware of an amazing fact: Bradley
and I hardly ever touch each other anymore. Long
ago, we used to punch and kick and tickle and yank.
We wrapped our arms around each other's necks and
walked like two drunks in the street, pulling each other from side to side and finally falling down.

But recently we touch with only words, our minds
meet and clasp but our flesh withdraws. It's no longer
safe to intertwine. The only thing he touches is my
hair, he has a way of pulling it and taking me with it.
My hair is the only safe part of me to touch.

So today, swimming in Sugar Creek, washing off
the mud and flies, floating on our backs and dreaming.
"You look like a whale," Bradley says, and I churn
the water and blow my spout.

"Don't do that, you'll get typhoid," he says, and
then he does exactly the same thing, filling his mouth
up with water and spitting it out. We are two whales,
kicking and thrashing and spouting typhoid germs. And
then Bradley, like a sounding fish, dives deep and
catches my ankles, turns me over so that I see silver
skin, churned mud, lose my breath and come up sput-
tering and coughing.

"Hey Apple, I'm sorry, are you okay?" He pulls

me toward the bank, and I climb out, laughing and choking. And he has to slap me on the back and squeeze out my hair. He says, "Artificial respiration," laughs, touches my shoulder, slides his wet hand down my wet arm to my fingertips. Touching.

We stand together for a long time, time to let the breeze dry us, time to let the world happen over and over again, time to let the trees settle their limbs and sigh, and in a hundred-year journey Bradley's body travels closer to mine. We are so close together, I can feel his shape from top to bottom and yet he is hardly leaning toward me. And I hardly know what I am thinking, except that this closeness of him is so different from any other nearness, the smell of his hair, the salty scent of his skin so different from the Bradley apart from me. And his heart beating interferes with my own pulse, makes my own heart skip its rhythm and switch to the sound of Bradley's blood.

"We better go," he whispers. A voice quiet on my mind, a sound protecting me from things I don't even know might happen. Soft breath brushing past my nose. His toes step on mine and we bump knees. The moment for speaking is gone. We are once again apart. Bradley. Alexandra. Two strangers arranging their clothes. Two friends again, pushing off into the water, rowing away.

I feel like I've been filmed in slow motion. The oars go languidly in and out of heavy water. We move through molasses. And then something flashcracks past the outermost rim of my mind's eye. "What was that?" I ask.

Bradley's eyes dart toward the hill. "Nothing." But there, behind the trees, Pan is lurking, cloven hooves shod with shoes. A rippling tripping laughter whips through my bones.

Oh go to sleep, Alexandra, I tell myself, stop scaring yourself to death. Go to sleep and wait for another day.

In the morning everything is wrong. I oversleep, for

one thing, and the sound of the telephone ringing wakes me up. The sky is gray and I remember I have to go down to Haight & Roth's to buy a record album for my cousin Annie which reminds me that we have to drive over to Stillwater on Saturday and celebrate Annie's birthday which means sitting around in a dress doing nothing while my mother admires Annie's mother's new rug or new curtains or new flowerpots or whatever is new on the agenda. My aunt and uncle are always redecorating and talking about what they're going to get rid of next. And they always tell the price of everything. When I go to the kitchen my mother is in a weird mood. She's already put all the breakfast dishes in the dishwasher and she's dressed.

"Good morning," I say, trying to cheer up the day.

"Good morning, Sandy," my mother says, very stiffly and very pointedly. Good morning is not the type of thing we usually say to each other in the morning so I guess we both are a little surprised.

I get out my organic wheat flakes and pour them into a bowl. My mother starts wiping off the front of the refrigerator. Something angry and sad is in the air.

"I'm going right down to Haight's this morning," I tell her, hoping it will make her feel better.

"That's a good idea," my mother says like it's the worst idea she's heard in years. Our conversation falls flat on its face. I eat my wheat flakes, munching away, wincing at every crunch. I never noticed how wheat flakes could sound so loud. My mother keeps on wiping the refrigerator. Tick tick, tock tock goes the battery clock on the wall. That means it's going to need a new battery very soon.

"Should I get a new battery for the clock?" I ask, still trying to get rid of the atmosphere by being helpful.

"You're in a helpful mood this morning," my mother says.

What's the matter, Mom, I want to ask, aren't you feeling all right? But something stops me from asking the question. Something tells me I don't want to know the answer. All of a sudden, wheat flakes taste like cardboard.

"I don't want you hanging around with Bradley so much anymore," my mother blurts out.

The bottom falls out of my stomach. I don't want to look at wheat flakes ever again in my whole life. "Why not?" I ask. And I feel so angry, angrier than I thought I was before I asked.

"I'm not going to get into a discussion about it right now, Sandy," my mother says. "I want you to spend more time with your other friends. The other girls have . . ."

"Why not? Why not? What's wrong all of a sudden?"

"Don't interrupt me . . ." But I don't give her a chance to speak. "I think it's ridiculous I think it's unfair," I say and I feel my insides shaking. "It's very unfair."

My mother takes a blue-and-white mug off one of the hooks under the shelves and pours coffee into it from the electric percolator. Her movements are slowly deliberate. She tilts the plastic bottle of Sucaryl and taps out measured drops.

"Bradley's in trouble with the police again," she says. "I don't understand why that boy has to wander around in the middle of the night," she murmurs. And I see the regret between her words. It's like she's saying: Bradley, why can't you be the way I think boys should be, why can't you be conventional, ordinary, the same old usual, why can't you act right so I wouldn't have to tell Sandy not to hang around with you?

And inside me, one kind of anger is replaced by another. The point about Bradley is that he is not ordinary, not usual, not conventional. He's different. And adults can't stand it if you're different. They get nervous, I guess, it makes them question their own way of life. I feel so angry at everybody for making Bradley into some kind of freak. I feel as if it's me and Bradley against everybody else. "Why don't they just leave him alone?"

My mother. stirs her coffee. She doesn't know why they don't just leave him alone. I don't even think the police know why. Bradley doesn't do anything when he takes a walk at night. It's just that he has all this creative energy and he can't sleep. He climbs out his bedroom window and he takes a walk. An innocent walk. But the police are always bugging him. There must be worse things going on in the world, but in Ravanna River it's a serious crime to do anything that people don't understand. It doesn't make any sense to the police that Bradley enjoys taking a walk at three A.M. It irritates them. "Kids" are supposed to be asleep at three o'clock in the morning, is what they say. "Hey Kid," they call Bradley, and they want to know what he's up to. When he tells them he's simply taking a walk they laugh. Hey Kid, they say, what are you? Some kind of nut?

I get up from the table and dump the rest of my wheat flakes into the garbage can.

"I mean it, Sandy," my mother says.

"When did he get in trouble? I just saw him yesterday."

"Last night. They took him back and woke his parents up. I don't think those people even know what their own child is doing half the time. They were asleep and he's out walking around the neighborhood."

"News sure does travel fast," I say sarcastically. It's only 9:43 on the wall clock. *Tick* tock tick *tock* it goes, letting us know it's running out of time.

"Mrs. Trahey called me." Mrs. Trahey is a friend of my mother's who lives on the same street Bradley does. I always suspected Mrs. Trahey kept my mother posted on what was going on at Bradley's house. I mean, my mother always seems to know when to call there when I'm late. Mrs. Trahey is the resident spy on that street. She was probably up at three A.M. herself. I always disliked Mrs. Trahey but now I hate her. She's the kind of person who lives in the dark. She says it's to save on electricity but now I know the real reason she turns all the lights off. It's to fool people into thinking there's no one home. It's her camouflage. You walk past Mrs. Trahey's house and you never suspect she's inside, lurking behind the living-room drapes, putting her evil eye on you.

"Where are you going?" my mother asks.

"I'm going down to Haight's."

"I'm sure Bradley's parents are having enough trouble without your barging in," my mother says. "Please remember what I said, Sandy. I don't want you going over there today."

"I'm going to Haight's, I told you."

I stomp out of the kitchen and bang the door when I go out. Halfway down the street I'm sorry I even bothered to slam a door. It's not worth it. Bradley never does things like that. He's always calm and collected. He doesn't waste his time and energy on foot-stomping and door-slamming. He knows what's important in life. Three quarters of the way down the street I remember that I forgot my wallet. I debate whether to go back and lose face or ask Haight's to charge the record. My parents have a charge account at Haight & Roth's but they never like to use it. I'm never supposed to use it, especially after I once charged a whole lot of paperbacks that I felt I couldn't live without. But I guess it will be all right to charge a record for once. After all, it's for my cousin, not for me.

Haight's is practically empty in the back where the phonograph records are. Up front it's always busy with people buying newspapers and magazines and cigarettes and stationery. But in the back they have records and stereo sets and radios and cameras and nobody is buying those this morning.

I start flipping through the record albums, not really feeling very enthusiastic, and Mr. Roth comes over and asks if I need any help. "Cheer up, don't look so glum," he tells me. "It's a beautiful morning out in the world."

Suddenly I want to tell him about Bradley and me and the police and my mother. But that's stupid. Mr. Roth, nice as he seems, doesn't really care about my problems. So I go back to looking at the records, trying to make my face do what it doesn't want to do, trying to cheer up for Mr. Roth. After about half an hour of making no decisions I bring my uninspired choice to the counter.

"Sure you won't try a little Bach? Beethoven? What about Brahms?" He gets out his book when I tell him I want to charge it. "Not that I don't appreciate a little acid rock now and then," he says, and winks. "Would you like it gift-wrapped?" he asks, as if he knows I wouldn't dare charge a record album for myself.

"Yes please," I say, because Haight & Roth's has really nice gift-wrapping and it will eliminate the need for my mother to make comments like "What's this?" and "I don't think Annie listens to this stuff, Sandy," etc., etc., etc.

When I get back out in the street it feels strange. Because my first thought was to go to Bradley's house and then I remember that I'm not supposed to hang around with him so much sandy.

Do you believe in fate? ESP? There I was, standing in the street in front of Haight's, feeling absolutely like I wanted to see Bradley more than anything else in the world. And there was Bradley. Appearing out of my mind's hoping, my heart's yearning, standing suddenly in front of me, wearing his shirt from the day before and his cut-off Levi's and his hair shining in the sun.

"Apple, are you tripping?" he asks and laughs. "You're tripping on the morning air, Apple, I've been talking to a stone wall for five minutes."

"You were not, where did you come from?"

"I came from Chichen-Itza," he says. "Come on."

"Where are we going?"

"Who knows, let's walk, let's go to my house, I'll read you the latest chapter of my book."

"I can't."

I don't have to explain to Bradley what I can't means. He knows I don't mean I can't, I have to go to the dentist, he knows I mean I can't, I'm not supposed to see you. A shadow, the dark wings of an owl flying past the moon, clouds that eat the sun, doubt slinking past Bradley's eyes. For the first time I see the features of his face fade into tiredness, as if he's been too long in the world's wind, the clear energy of his fine features vanishing. He's sick of fighting back. "See you, Apple," he says and walks away.

Bradley Bradley *Bradley,* my dumb heart screams. But I have old lead feet, weighed down by parental stones, stupid feet that take too long to decide to run after him.

Sometimes you feel as if nothing can get worse, that you've reached rock bottom and the only way to go is up. At least, that's the way I felt on the way home.

Didn't I say I was an optimist? What a stinking morning, I thought, what a putrid, rotten, lousy day. But underneath I knew I was waiting for a change for the better. Maybe I imagined I'd walk into my house and my mother would say: Surprise, I don't care if you see Bradley in fact why don't you see Bradley always forever every minute and by the way, why not take a few walks at three A.M. yourself? Optimists are absolute fools, I found that out. When I walked into my house my mother had a surprise, but it wasn't anything optimistic, in fact, it gave me a case of Instant Cynic.

"Sandy," she said, in a tight white voice, giving me the foreboding shakes, "I want to talk to you." And I thought, how could she have found out so soon, how could she be angry with me for just talking to him for five seconds on the street? But life wasn't finished giving me surprises.

"What were you thinking of?" my mother said. "How could you do such a thing?" How can a voice be alive and dead at the same time? How can it sound like screaming and be so quiet?

"Mom, Mom, what are you talking about?" And my legs feel watery, my stomach feels guilty without knowing why.

"You and Bradley . . . in the woods! Sandy, what a terrible thing to do."

What did I do? Is touching forbidden? Do I get a life sentence for feeling love? Are they going to tie me up in an electric chair and punish me with dying for wanting to be held?

THREE

Eyes swollen. Voice gone. Soul parched and tired of defending itself. My parents won't believe Bradley and I did not have, as they can hardly say through their angry lips, "sexual intercourse." I don't care anymore whether they believe me or not. Let them think what they want to think because the joke's on them. It's not the first time Bradley and I were together like that. We did the same thing last fall, when we swam in the pond behind the Staneblood house. But there's no sense in trying to convince your parents about a thing like that. Even if they say they believe me, they'll go on privately thinking exactly what they want to think. So let them.

I'm glad I started writing a journal because it's sort of comforting to write in it at a time like this. I turned on the radio and Debussy was playing, very softly. Mr. Roth would be glad.

Quartet in G, In the Trees
    She realized as he left, his angry good-bye only a plaintive searching for a place in her memory. And she wanted to promise, from a heart rent with its own demolition, quickly before the cement of time sealed up the wounds, promise him that they would never again go separate journeys. But ever remain in succinct sameness, two

beings within one life, two lives within one being.

The problem is how to get in touch with Bradley. I
want to talk to him *now* but there's no chance. My
parents are on guard duty in the living room, just
waiting for the Prisoner to make a move. They
wouldn't let me use the telephone to call my grandmother, no less Bradley. And anyway, who knows
what's going on at Bradley's house. I'd like to imagine that his parents would be a little more reasonable
than mine. I doubt it though. He's probably getting
screamed at too. The one thing there's no doubt about
is the fact that they've heard the big news of B. and A.
at Sugar Creek. If my parents didn't tell them you can
be sure someone like Mrs. Trahey did. For all I know,
Mrs. Trahey was the creep who told my mother in
the first place. When she's not hiding behind the
drapes of her living room, she's probably out slinking
along the banks of Sugar Creek on the lookout for
vice and sin. Why can't people just mind their own
business? Everybody is always worrying about what
everybody else is doing. The real reason my parents
are upset is because they're worried about what other
people will think. It seems like all their opinions are
based on what the neighbors think. I'd like to know
what they would say if there were no neighbors. I'd
like to know if they really care one way or the other,
deep down, inside themselves.

My mother is worried about my job. Next week I'm
starting work at the day-care center, helping out with
lunch and taking the kids swimming in the afternoon.
I guess she thinks they won't want me working there,
like I might corrupt the children's morals or something.
God, I feel so tired. Now I know how Bradley felt this
afternoon when I said "I can't." He must be absolutely exhausted with life. How many times, after all, can
you be bothered explaining you're only taking a walk?

The Debussy is over. Now they're playing piano

music, a long black dirge, nothing happy about it. Or maybe I'm incapable of hearing the happiness right now. Sometimes Bradley plays the piano by the window in his living room. He knows how to play all kinds of classical pieces but he prefers improvisational jazz. Bending his body forward, sort of humming with his fingers, he takes off on a far-out theme. Or he'll explain as he plays, things I can't understand, twelve tones, fractured rhythms, prehistoric folk songs. His mother calls out, "Bradley, I'm trying to think."

He closes the piano very carefully. His whole countenance looks out of place in his mother's beige-and-white velvet living room, a place where fugues are spoken, never sung, as he says. His mother is always nagging him not to get mud and dirt on the white carpet. I don't blame him for not wanting to play the piano very much.

I wish I could see him now. Talk to him now. Tell him that I'll never say "I can't" again. But as I'm debating how I'll fit through my bedroom window, how I'll climb out and run to Kenworth Avenue, my mother walks in. Of course she always knocks politely first but then she just opens the door. What's the point in knocking if you're only going to barge in anyway? "Come in," I tell her. She ignores that.

"Sandy," she says, "your father thinks you should go away to camp."

Camp! Camp is lower than low on the list of things to do this summer. Not only that, I was counting on the money from my job. The Jaffes always go away in the summer and I lose my baby-sitting income. I sit for them a lot in the winter, usually on Friday and Saturday nights, when they go out to dinner parties. They're the heads of the Ravanna River Friends of the Arts and there's always something going on for them to go to.

"I don't particularly want to go to camp," I tell my mother.

"Your father thinks it's a good idea." My mother

nods her head up and down like a marionette. Yes
yes yes yes, a good idea.

"What the hell kind of camp am I going to go to at
my age?" I yell. But my mother ignores that too. She
keeps her voice reasonable and calm. She refuses to
be incited to riot.

"There are some very good camps," she says.
"There's a riding camp up in Exeter and there's also a
drama camp for girls your age. We can look into them
tomorrow. It's late but maybe we can find one that has
room."

"I'm not going."

My mother and I stare at each other across my
room. She's wearing her blue jeans with the pink shirt
I hate. It makes her look fat and she's really not fat at
all. All her makeup is off, except for the black smudges
under her eyes from mascara. I keep looking at her
and trying to realize she's my mother. It's like looking
at a stranger, it's like looking at a word you've seen
and used a million times and one day it suddenly seems
weird and unrecognizable.

"I'm not going to discuss it anymore tonight," my
mother says. "We'll make a few calls in the morning."

"I don't care what you say . . ." but she's already
closing the door on my words, "I'm not going. *I'm not
going!*" Oh, what's the use. When I was a little kid I
used to get mad and throw my toys all over the room,
messing up the place on purpose. That kind of thing
is pretty pointless now. I'm the one who will have to
clean it up. So I just stay sprawled on my bed, feeling
as grouchy as possible, cooking up a nice big pot of
rage. God, I wish I could talk to Bradley.

Maybe I'll pray. Pray for him to climb out his window and come over to see me. He knows which one
my bedroom window is. He could sneak through the
side hedge and get the garbage can to stand on. He
could tap very softly on the glass and I'd hear him.
Then I would climb out and we'd walk all over Ravanna River together, we'd walk up and down every
street and tell all the cops to drop dead.

How do you pray for something impossible like that? Unless it's the right kind of prayer, you can't expect an answer. But don't ask me what the right kind of prayer is, you have to ask God. As far as I can tell, his answers are all according to the mood he's in, or maybe he just has specified times for tuning in and answering prayers and if you're lucky you get on the right wavelength. Once I prayed that I would find my wallet that I'd lost at the movies. I prayed so hard my eyes started to burn and I found the wallet. But another time I prayed that I would find my new five-dollar sunglasses at the beach and I never did. If you're not careful, you end up believing that wallets are more important than sunglasses. My philosophy is: Don't count on praying for solving your problems.

I guess I believe in God. I mean, I'm not overly religious or anything but I'd like to think there was somebody or something around in the end. It's a kind of horrible and lonely feeling to think that absolutely *nothing* exists out there. Bradley believes that the human race hasn't even come close to what's really going on in the universe. He believes in more than God which he says is just a title, a name, a word. He believes in a universal super-something that we can't even begin to imagine with our small brains. That's okay with me, as long as there's *something*.

I suddenly realize the radio is full of static and some commentator has been babbling on for the last half hour. I turn the radio off and the house is very quiet. Maybe my parents have gone to bed, exhausted by their daughter.

I'm hungry. If I don't get something to eat I'm going to die. But I can't believe it. How can I be hungry and angry at the same time? And sick and frightened and disgusted. But hungry all the same.

Sneaking out into the dark hall. The lights are off in the living room. I tiptoe toward the kitchen, watching out for the floor near the linen closet which always creaks. I'm just about to push in the swing door to the kitchen when I hear their voices. The low drone of serious conversation. My mother is doing all the talking. "Yes, Frank, I know," she says, "but I still think camp is the best idea. She'll be completely away from here, it will give the thing a chance to blow over."

"Hand me a match, will you," my father says. His voice pauses and I can hear the snap of the match as he strikes it.

"Do what you want to do," he says, "you will anyway." He sounds angry.

Dishes rattle. ". . . Frank . . . for once . . . will you please?" my mother says, but I can't hear all the words.

"I have the convention next week. I can't just cancel out."

"Well, I'm going to send her to camp," my mother's voice says. The dishes are quiet now. Her voice is throbbing.

"It's your idea," my father says. He coughs. A chair scrapes. "Christ," his voice says near the door, and he coughs again.

Hey what are you talking about? I want to scream. Who says what and who is who? "Your father's" idea has suddenly become my mother's and my father has a convention and really can't be bothered.

I don't know whether to laugh or cry. How many of my father's ideas have been my mother's? At first I feel like I should be mad at my mother for lying but then I get even angrier at my father. Doesn't he have any ideas of his own? If he doesn't think camp is so hot how come he doesn't make another suggestion? And anyway, whose life is it? Do they think I'm just some dumb puppet who can be danced around and told any old thing?

This place is suffocating me. The walls clamor. They don't know. They don't understand.

My father's coughing sends me running back to my room. My appetite is gone. I want to fly from this framework prison. I want to be free.

Once I read that if you wish for something hard

enough it surely happens. Is wishing the same as praying?

Oh I wish I could be music, spinning, turning, twisting, disappearing in the air.

FOUR

Bradley walks on the surface of the moon. His silver boots kick moondust, his arms swim in an airless void. He calls and the sounds of his voice come out of his heart. Apple, Apple, I'm going Awaaaaaaay.

I wake up, shaking. My legs are shivering under the sheet. It's the middle of July and I'm freezing to death. Ugh, what a horrible nightmare, worse than the one I had last night about my teeth falling out. Then I remember what I'm going to do. I push my arm into a shaft of moonlight and look at the time on my watch. In an hour I'm going to meet Bradley and Taylor and we're going across to South Haven, the town below Stillwater, and we're going to hitch a ride. Bradley and me, that is, Taylor will be coming back.

Tomorrow morning when my mother comes in to wake me up I'm not going to be here. Alexandra Appleton will no longer be a resident of her room, her house, the town of Ravanna River. My suitcases are packed and stacked near my bedroom door, crammed with last-minute purchases of white blouses and green shorts, bathing suits and a pair of riding boots. The boots were expensive. My mother told my father she was "appalled" at the price. I don't know much about riding but tomorrow I am supposed to get on the train and go to the riding camp in Exeter for the rest of the summer. They took me on some special dispensation because my mother nagged them so much and my father called a friend of a friend of his whose daughter goes there every summer.

But tomorrow morning I won't be in my bed. All the white blouses and green shorts are going to be bereft of body. The riding boots will mourn lost feet. Maybe my mother can return them to the store.

I feel under my pillow for the alarm clock and I push in the switch to turn off the alarm. I'm glad I won't have to let it ring, I was worried about waking my parents up. I didn't really think I'd fall asleep but Bradley was right. He said to go to bed as usual and try to get some rest. We aren't leaving until four-thirty. That way we'll be out on the highway by five-thirty or six. He says it won't look so unusual for us to be hitching early in the morning. It won't make everybody immediately suspicious the way it would in the middle of the night. Bradley should know, he's had enough experience with being bugged at night.

I didn't know until yesterday that I was running away. Up until then I felt depressed and hopeless. Things hadn't improved around my house in the past week. I guess I didn't help much, either. I kept having stupid arguments with my mother about nothing. Like whether or not I spilled the soap powder under the sink, or did I wash out the bathtub the last time I used it, or where was my white summer skirt that I haven't seen since last September. One day I got so disgusted I just left the house, screaming that I was going to Bradley's whether she liked it or not. She came after me in the car and we had a big scene right in the middle of Ravanna Avenue. My mother says she's never going to forgive me for embarrassing her in front of all the neighbors. But it wasn't all my fault. She shouldn't have come after me. There we were, my mother saying "Yes you will get in the car," and me saying "No I won't get in the car," and neither one of us budging an inch. I can't believe she didn't realize how ridiculous it was. But I guess it was the kind of thing where once she started she had to stay and finish. And she won in the end anyway. I got in the car. Bradley wouldn't have been home at any rate. I remembered later that he had some kind of job in Stillwater. His father arranged it for him instead of his working at the daycare center with me. We wouldn't have seen each other very much anyway since Bradley was going to be in the recreational center. But our parents couldn't take a chance. After all, we might forget ourselves in a moment of passion and tear off all our clothes and start carrying on in front of all the little kids. Well, it was all a waste since my mother made arrangements with the riding camp and called up the center and told them that unfortunately I wouldn't be able to work there because this wonderful opportunity had come up and she was sure they would understand that I had to take it. Instead of making things better adults always make things worse. Now everybody is gossiping about the big B. and A. scene. They're thinking all the things that my parents were so anxious for them not to know.

Last night I felt about as hopeless as anyone could get. After the dream about my teeth all falling out I woke up and felt scared. The house was making strange sounds, creaking and groaning and snapping and for the first time in a long while I started thinking about ghosts and horrors and fiends. I mean I knew it was stupid but I just lay there in bed, afraid to look at the black oblong space between my door and the jamb, and I was afraid to move a muscle in case *it* was looking at me from the hall. *It* was the face of the night, the spirit of darkness, the trembling shadow-figure that smears itself across the lawn at midnight. I didn't even want to get up to go to the bathroom. It was like I was a child again, afraid of the dark. I used to like my mother to leave a light on in the hall all night so in case I woke up I wouldn't be afraid. But I haven't had the light on in the hall for years. What got into you, Alexandra? I asked myself, are you some kind of nut being afraid to go to the bathroom in your own damn house?

So I tried to convince myself that there was nothing to be afraid of and that the real reason I was getting panicked was camp, and not seeing Bradley for six or seven weeks. And then I told myself to look at the bright side, that I'd be coming back and starting school and I'd be able to see Bradley anytime I wanted to whether they liked it or not since we were in the same school, same class. But no sooner did I give myself this comforting message than I got panicked all over again and started worrying that Bradley would move away or my parents would sell the house. Then I really did have to go to the bathroom and I got up and crept through the black oblong nightmare door, sort of waiting for something to pounce.

Well, there's something mundane about a bathroom and flushing the toilet and all that cured me. I wasn't scared. So I brushed my teeth again, I guess to assure myself they hadn't really fallen out, and I took an aspirin and drank a glass of water and for some unknown reason I decided to look out the bathroom window. The window is small, high, set above the rose trellis. I turned out the light and stood up on my toes and pulled the curtains back.

And there, out on Ravanna Avenue, looking like a lonely ghost, was Bradley. Unmistakable. But I thought I was dreaming again. What do you do when you want to make sure you're alive and awake? Pinch yourself, take your pulse? Count up the beating of your blood and see if there's any pain? My soul jumped, I wanted to leap right out the window.

Instead I ran to the front door, remembering too late that I was wearing my dumb yellow shortie pajamas. But I didn't care, I ran across the lawn, afraid to shout and afraid to be too late.

Our hands bumped, our bodies scraped sideways, we moved in wrong directions and had to right ourselves. Bradley. We stood there and gaped at each other, me in my dopey pajamas. We were so happy to see each other but a little uneasy with the joy. Two people who allegedly had sexual intercourse by Sugar Creek. The infamous two, the lascivious pair. He hugged me.

We had to whisper, How are you? What have you

been doing? Tell each other about my going to camp, about working in Stillwater. Everything. "I'm going away, Apple," he said. "I'm splitting. I can't take the hassling anymore." Those words frightened me more than any dark hallways could.

"But what have they done? What's going on?" There was no time to say it all. There was the nervous moonlight flickering in our eyes. The sound of cars far off but coming nearer. He put his hands on my shoulders and leaned over and kissed me. Not a kiss from a time before, not sloppy, nonsensical, fooling around smoochings, but the way we should have touched at Sugar Creek.

Wait a minute, take me with you, I thought, I'm already on that road, I can't turn around now. The sound of a car seemed to come closer. "You take care of yourself," he said, already moving away.

Mercurial visions, eyes in the back of my head, seeing my house, the half-mowed lawn, the split-rail fence my father and my uncle never finished putting up together.

If I stay, Bradley, I stay as part of you. Living only in the chasm you leave behind, a burrowed-out place, shafts of light where your thoughts and words remain.

"I'm going, too."

"No good, Apple."

Oh my dearest life, the wings and wind on which I ride. I am afraid of losing you, for then I lose part of myself.

"But how are you going? Where?"

Scrambles of the future turn in my mind, as Bradley explains about getting Taylor to take him across to South Haven the next night, about hitching, about his friend in a place called New Life.

"You can't tell me not to come."

"No," he says, "I can't tell you not to come."

I get up now and pull on my blue jeans, put on a shirt, roll up a sweater and scarf and socks, put them in my knapsack with the rest of the things. I didn't dare pack it all before now, afraid my mother would find out.

I guess I do feel a little guilty about running away. My mother made a big thing about my taking the train to Exeter instead of her driving me up there. She didn't actually say it but I know she wanted to show that she trusted me. A lot of good trust does now! She thought it would prove that she didn't have to worry about me getting off someplace else and doing something foolish. Well, I did think of getting off someplace else and running away from there. But then I thought of the camp car waiting at the station for me and all the panic and confusion and my parents worrying about whether I'd been killed or kidnapped at Wallington where I had to change. Forget it, I thought, it's better to make it clear what I'm doing. So before I went to sleep I wrote them a note. I wrote about ten notes, actually, trying to decide exactly what to say. My note isn't very profound or poetic or anything. It still doesn't say what I want to say but I don't have the time or space to go into reasons. They wouldn't understand anyway.

My note says:

> Dear Mom and Dad (my father is away at a convention but I had to include him),
> I left last night. I know it's silly to tell you not to worry about me but I really wish you wouldn't because I'll be okay. I'll call you and let you know how I am. Please understand that I must go away and be me alone for a while. I plan to come back in time for school.
>
> Love, Alexandra

I don't really know if I plan to come back for school, but I put that in the note because I thought it might make my parents leave me alone. I don't know what happens when you run away since I've never done it before but I'm sure they'll call the police and all that. I only hope they can think of me being away just for the summer, like I was at camp. I hope they don't get carried away.

The last thing I put in my knapsack was my money. I went to the bank this afternoon and withdrew some from my savings account. I didn't dare take too much because I was afraid they would call my mother and ask her if it was all right. So I only took thirty dollars and I made a lot of dumb comments to the teller who was Mrs. Rogers, a friend of my mother's. I said I was going to camp and I wanted to have a little spending money, ha ha. I don't think she was even listening and she probably didn't give a damn. But I went at a quarter to three just in case my mother planned to go to the bank herself. I couldn't tell my mother I needed the money for camp because she had already given me ten dollars plus the money for my carfare and everything. I'm not supposed to withdraw money from my savings account. It's being saved for college.

I put my wallet into the zipper pocket in the knapsack. Then I unzipped the pocket and took it out again. Altogether I had fifty-eight dollars and fifty-nine cents. This included the carfare and ten dollars plus some babysitting money of my own. I held all the money in my hand for a while and thought about it and then I took fifteen dollars out and put the bills on top of the note on my desk. It wasn't fair to take all the camp money with me. It would just give my mother something else to be mad about.

I'm going.

I'm leaving.

I look around my room like a dying swan, feeling dramatic and foolish. Good-bye Everything. Good-bye Nothing. I realize that possessions don't matter. You can always buy new stuff. You can always replace the accouterments of life.

But you can't replace your soul. You can't go to the store and buy a new psyche.

I check the time. Open my window and throw my

knapsack out. Then I creep silently out of my bedroom, down the hall, holding my breath, ready with
my explanations if my mother wakes up. Will she believe that I'm just going out to watch the sunrise? Of
course she won't. She'll think I'm meeting Bradley to
say good-bye before I leave for camp. And maybe she
won't mind. Maybe she would even let me. And this
makes me feel guilty again. My mother can't help being my mother. She's stuck with the job. I guess she
thinks she's doing the right thing most of the time. I
guess I can't blame her. It's just that what she doesn't
understand is that she can't live my life for me. She
can't save me from all the things she's always trying to
save me from. A person has to do it all himself even if
he makes a mess of things.

My mother can't smile for me, be happy for me,
hurt for me. I have to find out for myself.

Good-bye Good-bye, and I'm out the door, around
the house, I have my knapsack on my back and I'm
gone.

Bradley and Taylor will be waiting at the river.

I run without losing my breath. It's like flying. And I
sing in Bradley's famous made-up language. Gone-
going spacialpot. Bonnelbom wondrufwom. Strum tum
lorrie gatheracker.

The air is clear.

I can live.

FIVE

Bradley and I are lying on our backs in a field. If we
don't look anywhere but up we can imagine we're in
the middle of nowhere, a faraway bucolic place popu-
lated with clouds and cows.

Actually, over to the right of the field is the highway. And off in the left are the distant smokestacks of
a factory. Wispy traces of black smoke left over in
the sky.

Bradley is talking about "being." One leg is crossed over the other and I can see his bare knee poking out through the rip in his jeans. He wags his toes as he talks. The truth inside, he says, is what creates your way of life, what makes you what you are, regardless of the label, in spite of whether you even have a label for it or not.

I keep falling asleep and missing words. I can't help it, I've never felt so tired in my whole life. It's like a sickness, this tiredness, it comes in ponderous waves, stuffing my mouth with heavy cotton, stopping up my ears with lumps of clay, dragging me across an endless sea of grassy sleep.

"*so . . . gow . . . lonnneeeeee,*" Bradley says, and I hear the constant swishswoosh of traffic in between the syllables. I try to force my eyes to stay open, try to concentrate on staying awake. But as I watch, Bradley's nose grows two lumps, enlarges, turns into a turnip, flies off his face and disappears. "Go to sleep, Apple," he says, and I feel the movement of his pushing the knapsack under my head to make a pillow.

Tired but at peace. As if a tightly twisted spring inside has sprung. It seems right for me to be lying on the ground, next to Bradley, in a place I've never been before. I sleep, dreaming gentle words, no more afflictions of lost teeth and wounded hearts. Pink-and-yellow sun warming me, moving across the sky and my body. The color of my dream is saffron, citron, xanthophyll.

Open my eyes. Feeling fine but stiff in the back. The sun has moved away. Bradley is sitting up, hugging his knees, looking across at the highway. He lifts his hand to his mouth, puts his index finger between his lips and bites his nail.

"Good morning."

"I've been thinking," Bradley says, and turns to face me, reaches over and brushes the hair out of my eyes. "We better hitch to Oak Brook and stay there a couple of days."

"Oak Brook?"

"My aunt and uncle live there."

Aunt Uncle Oak Brook? I don't understand what he's talking about. I thought we were running away. He explains to me and my ear is cocked, waiting to hear the synthetic substitutions, listening to an ersatz dream. They are not really his aunt and uncle but good friends, friends of the family who will put us up. Can you think of a better place to go, Apple? We can't just sleep in the middle of the highway. We'll stay there and get a ride to New Life. "I want to go to New Life," Bradley says. "I'd like to become part of the community there."

I try to understand but somehow I feel cheated. He's right, of course. We have no tent and only one sleeping bag, Bradley's. Maybe he's angry that I came along so unprepared. Maybe he's thinking: everything would be fine if I didn't have *her* with me, an extra human, a complication, a responsibility. I realize I know nothing about running away. I don't know the rules and regulations. I unrealistically imagined you just start running. But you have to know where you're running to. And you have to bring along the things that make the running smooth. Life always gets you with the trivia of living. You can't sleep on the sidewalk, you can't sleep on a park bench. Even in the state park you can only go to certain specified areas and you have to have a permit to do it.

"What are they going to say?" I ask Bradley.

"Nothing. You just come along with me. Okay?"

"Okay."

We pick ourselves up, Bradley puts on his sneakers, we start toward the highway. The cars go swizzing past, never stopping, never ceasing. Oak Brook is south. Bradley puts out his thumb. Swizz swizz nobody looks, nobody cares. Swizz swoosh screeech, somebody stops. A man in a blue truck. There's room in the cab to squeeze in two. "Where ya going?" he yells to Bradley.

"Oak Brook."

"Take ya there, pretty damn close at least. Hop in."

The back of the truck is empty except for a square white refrigerator turned on its side, partly covered with a large brown piece of burlap. The inside of the cab smells like stale cigars. Bradley slams the door and we take off with a big lurching grind. I'm squashed in the middle. Bradley has his arm and shoulder out the window to make more room. The gearshift keeps hitting my leg.

"So you kids bumming around?"

"We're going to Oak Brook," Bradley says.

"Yeah but whatta you doing? Making it cross-country?"

"No, we're just going to Oak Brook."

The man's eyes blink. He stares at the road. "Talkative types, huh?" he says sarcastically.

I feel my cheeks getting hot. I hope I'm not turning red. I hate it when I blush. I try to lean more on Bradley than on the man. But it's hopeless. I'm pinched in between both of them, I can't get away.

"You been hitching rides all the way?"

"Yes," Bradley says.

"You like a free ride, huh?" Bradley says nothing. I keep trying to think of something to change the subject.

"What's the refrigerator for?" I blurt.

"Ha!" the man exclaims, not a laugh, not exactly a sneer. "Listen, it's one big free ride as far as you're concerned, right?"

"We can get off here," Bradley says. Not once has he looked at the driver. His face seems calm, he isn't even breathing hard. But his lips are pinched, stretched over his teeth.

The man is silent for about sixty seconds. Then he speaks in an entirely different kind of voice, "AAwaa-aawwww, no hard feelings. You want to get to Oak Brook, I'm taking you. No sweat now."

Why do I suddenly feel like crying tears of gratitude? There's certainly no reason to feel so indebted to this unpleasant person who is only going to do what he offered to do in the first place. And he has made us pay our fare, in humiliating currency.

We continue the journey in silence. My nose grows accustomed to the smell of cigars. I feel drowsy and hot and rest my head on Bradley's shoulder. Bradley smells of heat and sweat, a much nicer smell than cigars.

"How's this?" And we get dropped off about two miles from Oak Brook. An efficient journey. Bradley says "Thanks," as we get out. The man says, "So long." We stand by the side of the road until the truck drives off. We feel used up.

Then we walk. The closer we get to Oak Brook the more nervous I feel. I'm wondering if Bradley's aunt and uncle are going to grab me, put me in a sack, deliver me back to Ravanna River post-haste. But I have to believe in what Bradley is doing. I have to believe in what he says. Come along with me, okay? Okay. If I can't believe in Bradley then I might just as well give up.

The house is set back from the dirt driveway. You can't see it until you're practically on top of it. A chicken-wire type fence, nailed to sagging old wood poles, follows the driveway, keeping in a pasture. Under the trees and in between the overgrown forsythia bushes are the wooly, fat shapes of sheep. It's like another world here, hard to believe it's so close to the center of Oak Brook which is full of launderettes and gas stations and liquor stores. I think maybe it's going to be all right with Bradley's Aunt Ev and Uncle Tim.

The house is red and low, some new, some old parts. The front door is white with a brass knocker in the shape of a cat. Bradley knocks. It seems like nobody's home. The evening is quiet. A breeze ripples silently through the trees. Around the side of the house I can see an empty hammock.

The soft chink of something delicate. Footsteps. A woman opens the door. She's wearing a blue-checkered cotton dress and a white apron with a big red apple for a pocket. Her hair is gray, pulled back into a kind of sloppy looking bun. One of her big gray hair-pins is almost falling out.

"Hello, Aunt Ev," Bradley says. His body shifts suddenly, as if he's feeling as nervous as I am.

"Well, Bradley," says Aunt Ev, not seemingly over-ly surprised to see him, "you've grown some since I saw you last. Look at the size of him! Oh come in, come in, what am I doing." She holds the door open wide and beckons us inside.

"This is Alex," Bradley says awkwardly.

"Hello, Alex," Aunt Ev extends her hand. I take it. Warm, soft, slightly damp. Maybe she's been wash-ing dishes.

The house smells of mothballs and spice cake. I like it. "We're a mess in the living room," Aunt Ev chatters, leading us, herding us like the sheep. "Tim is putting in some shelves and he's got the whole wall torn apart." She keeps us moving along even though she never touches us. "Come on out back, he's in the yard somewhere."

Passing the living room, I take a quick sneak look. It doesn't look that messy after all. And then we're in the kitchen which is knotty pine and has a double stainless-steel wall oven. Aunt Ev opens the screen door and calls, "Ti . . . im. . . . He's in the garden, you go on out and say hello. Drop that stuff here, drop it. That's it. Go on now." Chattering chattering, getting Bradley to take off his wet and sweaty shirt. "Cool off," she says. "Do you good."

I start to follow Bradley out the door but Aunt Ev says, "Alex, would you like to use the john?" Maybe I'm not presentable to meet Uncle Tim, so I take the hint and she shows me where the bathroom is. Once inside I start laughing because it seems so incongruous to ask a guest "Would you like to use the john?" My mother always says, "the powder room," or do you want to "freshen up." She always pretends you do ev-erything but go to the toilet when you're in a bath-room.

I look at myself in the mirror. Except for a sooty

nose and a greasy looking forehead I don't look too
bad. I suppose Bradley and Uncle Tim were going to
have a private encounter, and Aunt Ev had to think
of some tactful way to keep me from going out there
in the garden with them. All she had to do was say,
"Let Bradley go alone." People should be more open
about things like that, they should come right out and
say what they mean.

I wash my hands, wash my face, comb my hair and
brush my teeth. When I get back to the kitchen Aunt
Ev has put out cups and saucers and a cake on the
kitchen table. The table is in a corner, separated from
the rest of the kitchen with plants and shutters. "Store-
bought cake," Aunt Ev says. "I hate to bake in this
heat." I smile feebly. I feel ridiculous.

"Sit down," she says. "I put the coffee on. But maybe you want a sandwich? I have ham and liverwurst
and some tomatoes. Not from the garden, not yet,
they're all green. How about a sandwich?"

I realize I'm ravenous. "Okay," I say, "yes, please."
I have a flash vision of my mother shaking her head.
Your manners, Sandy, please mind your manners.

Sitting awkwardly on the edge of the wooden chair,
wishing Bradley would hurry the hell up and come
back inside. I don't know what I'm going to talk to
Aunt Ev about. I don't know what I'm going to say if
she starts asking me questions. And I wonder why she
doesn't seem more curious. Maybe it's all a plot. Maybe
any minute now my parents are going to drive up in a
car, come out shooting, yelling, "Sandy, are you in
there? We know you're in there! Come out with your
hands up."

"Where do you live, Alex?" Aunt Ev asks, making
me jump.

"Ravanna River." I search my mind for something
to add to that meager sentence but I can't think of a
thing. It seems rude. Those two words alone. There
must be something I can add to it. So I add, "The
same town as Bradley." God what a dumb remark.

"You two in school together?" Aunt Ev asks, but

she doesn't wait for an answer this time. "I always liked Ravanna," she goes on. "We used to live over there years ago. But Oak Brook's nicer for Tim. He can have his sheep. You know, Ravanna used to be where we went for the fireworks when I was a child. They had the biggest display you ever want to see every Fourth of July. Did they have it this year?"

Oh sure, I think, we had special fireworks on Ravanna Avenue at the home of Alexandra Appleton. "Uh uh," I mumble, my mouth full of liverwurst sandwich, "they don't have it anymore. I think somebody got killed."

"Killed?" Aunt Ev is shocked. Maybe that was the wrong thing to say, too serious a subject to bring up when we were just making polite conversation. And I wish I hadn't said it anyway since I realize I don't know anything about it. For all I know it's just a rumor. For all I know, it never happened.

"What happened?" Aunt Ev wants to know. "Who was killed?" I'm not sure of anything. It's like I have no opinion. I wonder where I ever heard the story in the first place. All my opinions are my mother's and father's, all my facts belong to them. And a lot of them are wrong, based on preconceived notions of the world, misinterpretations of life. I promise myself never to say anything again until I'm sure it's something from within me alone. Something I know about, not something I heard.

Voices in the backyard. Bradley and Uncle Tim coming in. Bradley introduces me. Aunt Ev introduces me. We shake hands and laugh. Uncle Tim calls me "little lady." He has a fat stomach and short arms. His hair is gray and, the most surprising thing, it's long. That is, long for an Uncle Tim but not as long as Bradley's. It will be all right, I think, as Uncle Tim steers us all back to the table and tells Aunt Ev to bring the coffee in a hurry, quick. Uncle Tim won't send me back to my parents. I feel as if I've known him forever. I feel as if he's my friend from another time, another world.

And then he ruins it all. After we've finished eating our cake and Aunt Ev has complained that we're going to spoil our appetites for dinner and she should have known better, Uncle Tim pushes his plate back and says, "Well what do you say? Want to give your folks a ring? Tell them you're okay?"

It's like the blow I've been waiting for. It's like it was too good to be true anyway. Worst of all Bradley says, "Yeah, I will."

"Tim . . ." Aunt Ev says.

"I'll talk to Howard, take it easy." He smiles at Bradley. "Tell him I can put you to work here just as easy as Stillwater."

Bradley laughs in a funny way, half a cough, half a choke. I look at Uncle Tim out of the corner of my eye. He looks very friendly, very trustworthy. But my mother is always saying that you can't tell anything by appearances. She's always reminding me that I shouldn't judge a book by its cover. Just because somebody looks nice, adults always warn, it doesn't necessarily mean they are. Adults must be very jaded. They spend so much time advising you not to be taken in by a person's good looks that they forget the converse is also true. People who don't look so good on the outside can be beautiful on the inside. I never hear any mothers warning their kids about that.

"Whenever you're ready," Uncle Tim says, "no rush." It sounds good. It almost makes me like him again. But this time with reservations.

Bradley and I go down to feed the sheep. "He keeps them all summer," Bradley explains, "and he has them butchered in the fall. They have blankets made out of the wool."

"That's nice," I say unenthusiastically. I look at the meek sheep faces and wonder how they like it. They take one look at me and turn around and run away. "What are we doing here anyway?" I ask. "How long are we going to stay here?"

"We're going to New Life," Bradley answers, tak-

ing my hand, feeling like the Bradley I knew before.
Getting him back again, it's scary how quickly he
seemed to change and slip away. And I think, I've always known Bradley in Ravanna River. I've never
known him anywhere else.

He holds my hand all the way back from feeding
the sheep. Yet I feel confused. What did I expect?
That nothing would be a problem, that we could eat
the air and survive in the myriad facets of our brains?
And then I think: I didn't think at all. I never thought
beyond the river. "Are you going to call your parents?"
I ask him.

He looks so pale that it frightens me. But perhaps
it's just the coming moon.

"I guess so."

"Then I'll call mine too."

I don't know if I comfort him. I don't know if I
should be here. I'm afraid to doubt my own heart's
beating. Bradley seems so alone. Do I touch him as
he touches me? Does he need me? Or, if I go, will I
set him free?

SIX

I've been thinking a lot about sex. I think the combination of Sandy and sex really scares my parents. And
I wonder why. It's not just the business about getting
pregnant or V.D. I know all about V.D. We had a
special symposium on it in school last year. We had
lectures, discussion groups and there was a film
about a girl who thought she had syphilis and was
afraid to go to the doctor. Her girl friend finally con-
vinces her to go and she finds out it isn't syphilis at
all but something else that's not very serious. The moral of the story is: Get All the Facts.

But aside from all the facts, adults are hung up
about sex in relation to their children. I know they

have their own private feelings about it which you never get to find out. My mother isn't that prudish underneath it all. I mean, she laughs at dirty jokes at parties, although she always adds, "Oh that's terrible," after she's finished laughing. And I see her giving my father a pinch now and then or she'll giggle in a certain way when he whispers something to her. So why is she so unrealistic when it comes to discussing it with me? Why does she put on this pseudo-horrific moralistic front? As far as my mother is concerned, sex is supposed to be this big secret that I can't have any interest in until the night after my wedding day.

Once I asked her if she had had premarital sexual relations and she said I was being "impertinent." I bet she did.

When I argue that society is changing and girls don't believe in remaining virgins interminably she gets mad. The closest she ever came to agreeing with me was once when she said, "Look, Sandy, when you're a working, self-supporting adult I can't tell you what to do. You can make your own decisions then."

I suppose that means that sexual freedom goes hand in hand with working for a living. Virginity ends when the rent is paid. But most of the time she says, "We'll discuss that day when we come to it," or "Give yourself time, Sandy, what are you in such a hurry for?"

I don't know whether I'm in a hurry or not. I guess I never really took it personally until recently. I mean, I said I agreed with the rest of my friends, I went along with them when we had these big discussions on losing your virginity. We used to have these sleep-over parties where everybody brought their own pillow and blanket and we sat up until four A.M. talking about boys and sex and sometimes smoking. Janet Drackman always brought a pack of Kents and a huge bag of M & M's. Somehow the combination always gave me a headache. And the next morning I went home with a stiff neck and a hideous taste in my mouth and worried about breaking out in pimples from eating all that chocolate. I don't even like M & M's!

Lying in bed in the spare room at Aunt Ev and Uncle Tim's, things like sleep-overs seem out of place, out of time. I remember myself as a sort of pathetic figure, a person who adopted opinions to become part of the crowd. I don't think I ever felt anything about what we talked about. I was enveloped in a protective cloud, still immature, a crysalid being with no conscious knowledge of the flight to come.

I lie here and wonder if Bradley and I will have premarital sexual relations. Not here, of course, but someday, somewhere, soon. He's out in the living room, sleeping on the couch. I wonder if he wonders too. Or does he already know?

I'm getting to a place in time I never thought about getting to. It just kept developing through all these years, the continuum of Bradley. I mean, I don't think that anybody in Ravanna River ever thought of him as being my "boyfriend," at least not up to now. We never fit into their self-imposed patterns of romanticism. We were just Bradley and Alex, little kids growing up. We never talked about "dates" or "going steady" the way other people talked. Only once, when we were about nine, did Bradley proclaim his feelings aloud. My cousin Annie lived in California then, and she came to spend a month of the summer with us. She had funny reddish brown hair that she wore in two long braids. Every morning my mother had to braid Annie's hair and she never could do it just right. One braid was always bigger or fatter or looser than the other one. After breakfast and the hair-braiding we went to the playground on Kenworth Avenue where Bradley would be waiting for us, hanging upside down on the climbing frame or lying prone under a see-saw. He was always there first, we never beat him. Annie would go right up to Bradley and say, "Bradley, how about you braid my hair?" And Bradley would say, "Your hair's braided." And Annie would say, "It's done wrong, you do it, Brad."

And Bradley would try. No matter how sloppy a job he did, Annie said, "That's better, Brad." On the way home for lunch I chastised Annie.

"Don't ask Bradley to braid your hair."

"Why not?"

"Because it's not fair to my mother. She'll feel bad when she sees your hair done over again."

But Annie never took my advice. I detested Annie. The longer she stayed, the more I wanted to yank those braids, pull her hair right out of her stupid head. I guess Bradley must have known. One afternoon when Annie was over on the swings and he and I were hanging upside down on the climbing frame, getting red in the face and deaf in the ears, he said, "She's okay but I like you best." He went on philosophically rebraiding Annie's hair. But it no longer mattered to me. I was the one he liked best. A secret I kept warm inside of me. I felt vastly superior to Annie.

The world keeps turning, the days spin out your life and breath. Somewhere along the way Bradley named me Apple. He grew hair on his arms and legs and a fine soft down on his upper lip. His crooked tooth fell out and the new one that grew in was straight. He stopped having earaches every winter and his appendix was removed, an emergency on Thanksgiving Day which Bradley was very proud of. He was about to pull his trousers down to show everybody his scar when Miss Mulvihill, the fifth-grade teacher, caught and stopped him. All of those Bradleys have moved with me in time, so closely meshed with my life that I never even saw the change from boy to man.

And now I keep asking myself what makes one human being love another. I can find no logical explanation for the way my mind and body are suddenly existing only in relation to Bradley. It is the most complicated, mysterious, inexplicable thing in the world, this fact that I love him beyond everything, in a totality that confounds and overwhelms me. He is my world.

I wrote in my journal before I went to bed:

July's Journey
  Always before me, always behind, always within, racing in my mind. The trees are like the
jungle now, the air is hot. I am Clytie, I will turn
my face to follow you always. But if you pick
me, will I die?

It's hard to sleep here. The house makes strange
noises. The sheets smell different from the sheets at
home. These are full of sunshine and hot irons. Aside
from the time we stayed in a hotel one vacation, I've
never slept on ironed sheets. My mother had perma-
nent-press ones that she takes out of the dryer and
folds up. When I turn on my stomach I can hear my
heart beating through the mattress. Thump, thump,
thump, it tells me I'm living and breathing. I'm afraid
and happy at the same time. If it weren't for the fact
that I'm going to have to make a telephone call tomorrow I could almost believe in total joy.
  Why does it take so long to grow up?

SEVEN

Excerpts from a Telephone Duet, Ravanna River Ex-
hortations with very few variations on a theme:

  "Sandy, are you listening to me? Why are you doing this? Sandy, your father wants you to come home."
My mother sings across the wires, a disembodied voice
that sounds only vaguely familiar. "What are they
like? Are they nice people? They are nice people,
aren't they? Are you helping out? Please offer to help
with the dishes, Sandy, and try to pick up after yourself. As much as I disapprove, it's very nice of them
to do this. I'll have to write and thank them. Where
do you sleep? They are supervising, aren't they? Sandy,

tell me now, are they nice people?"

Please don't write any letters, Mom, please don't do anything except leave us alone. I sleep in a bedroom, cloistered in stiff white sheets, two angels at my right hand: Aunt Ev and Uncle Tim.

"I hope you and Bradley aren't going to do anything foolish. You have your whole life ahead of you, Sandy. Don't let one mistake ruin it. We can forget what happened. There's no need for you to take it all out of proportion."

"Mom, what are you talking about?"

The voice pauses. The silence waits for my mother to debate, to summon the courage to say: "You're not going to get married are you? Sandy?" My mother is afraid of all the wrong things. I wish I could convince her. She's spending all her time angry at things I never did, afraid of what I never thought of doing. "The reason we're not coming over there is your father thinks you can make the right decision on your own. We expect you to make the right decision, Sandy. We're not going to drag you home bodily. Your father expects you to do what's right. He expects you to come home."

"Do you miss me, Mom?"

"Sandy, what kind of thing is that to ask at a time like this? I don't know what's the matter with you. Don't you know just how much aggravation this has caused? I had to call the camp and they weren't too pleased after making a special effort to get you in. And I won't be getting the deposit back and I can't blame them. Oh Sandy, I don't know why this had to happen."

"Does Dad miss me?"

"Of course he misses you. He wants you to come home."

"Let me talk to him." In the silence I hear a sound I should recognize. It tantalizes my brain. Snap. Snap. A match striking a matchbook. The exhalation of smoke. My mother hardly ever smokes. It means she's very nervous.

"Hey Mom, hello?"

"Yes, I'm here."

"Can I talk to him?"

"He's not here now, Sandy."

"Doesn't he want to talk to me?"

"Of course he wants to."

"Then let me talk to him." I feel myself hurtling down a path to the answer I already know. I want to make myself hear it. Perhaps I want reasons to go on making my parents hurt. Perhaps I need a reason to do what I'm doing. And in a moment of painful insight a voice in my brain asks me coldly, Don't you already have the reason? Isn't Bradley the reason?

"He's in Chicago, the convention is on this week."

What? What did you say Mom? Did you say that my father wanted me to come home, my father is upset over his long lost daughter. Well, I guess he could be upset on the telephone from Chicago. But why can't he tell me himself. Why is it always Mom, the liaison, the go-between, father-daughter cementer. I realize that I don't know anything about the way my father feels. He never tells me anything. He speaks through my mother's lips and there's no way of my knowing which words are his and which are hers. Sandy, your father thinks you look lovely in that dress. Sandy, your father doesn't like your hair hanging in your eyes, your father doesn't want you to stay out later than eleven, your father thinks you should go to camp.

Sometimes Bradley sings a song, "You Upset the Grace of Living When You Lie," a Tim Hardin song that's too hard to sing so it comes out cracked, broken, incurably sad.

"That's better, isn't it?" Uncle Tim wants to know when I hang up, "It's always better to talk things out."

Maybe, but listen, Uncle Tim, it seems to me that instead of talking anything out I've talked things into my mind that I never considered thinking before.

I don't know what Bradley's parents said to him on the phone. Mostly Bradley just said Yes, No, Hmmm;

they did all the talking. But I do know that they're not coming to drag Bradley home bodily either. And I see them, Bradley's parents, my parents, Uncle Tim and Aunt Ev, arranging our mistakes to their own benefit, humoring our rebellion, complacently stroking their infinite wisdom and allowing us to play it on their terms.

The evening takes on the aspects of a surrealistic dream. We sit in the living room: Aunt Ev crocheting, Uncle Tim watching television, Bradley slunk in a chair with a book in his lap, me taking my cues from Aunt Ev, listening to her explanations of hooks and loops, learning the intricacies of the double crochet. We are going fast on the road to nowhere.

"Raspberries," Aunt Ev says, "isn't this yarn the color of raspberries?" And she whips the yarn around her fingers, hook hook hook, faster than I can follow. "Wonderful raspberries up on the hill," she says. "Remember how they grow near the tower?"

"Hmmmm," says Uncle Tim not paying any attention.

"You remember that tower, don't you, Bradley?" Aunt Ev asks.

Bradley has been off in another place. He rouses himself enough to shake his head.

"Don't you? We took you up there a couple of years ago. You complained the whole time that it was too long a walk and Uncle Tim finally had to carry you."

"That was more than a couple of years ago, Ev," Uncle Tim says, paying attention after all.

"Oh whenever," Aunt Ev says, huffily. "Now do you remember?"

"Is it still there?" Bradley asks.

"Sure. Wonderful view. I wonder if the raspberries are ripe. The birds get them if you don't pick them right away."

"What kind of tower?" I ask, only half interested. But Aunt Ev is back to her crocheting. Uncle Tim is laughing. They don't hear me.

I try to imagine what it would be like to be their child. They do all the things my parents do: cook meals, work in the yard, drive to the supermarket, make the beds, eat, sleep, eat, work. I wonder if they make love or are they too old?

And I wonder if that's the big secret. That life is just a dull nothing, eating and sleeping and cooking and cleaning with a little sex thrown in. Maybe that's why adults want to keep it a mystery. They're so embarrassed because they were taken in themselves. They can hardly admit to each other that they've been cheated, you can't expect them to admit it to their children.

I make myself a promise that it will never happen to me. Bradley and I will go on and on, experiencing the world, loving each other without drudgery. As long as I have him, I can find out what life is all about. We'll never allow ourselves to be constricted by the repetitious patterns of society's making. We'll always be free. "Bradley," I call telepathically, "Bradley, listen, we have to get out of here."

Bradley shifts in his chair, closes the book and puts it back on the coffee table. He turns and smiles at me. The smile says: Be patient, Apple, wait around and I'll be ready soon.

"Welllpppppp," Uncle Tim says, leaning forward and switching off the TV set, "time for bed." I look at my watch, amazed that it's almost twelve. Another day passing, another bit of soul lost.

"You comfortable out here, Brad?" they ask him. Bradley nods, yeah sure, don't worry about it.

I pause, wanting to stay with Bradley, wanting to be alone with him for a little while. But somehow Aunt Ev ushers me out. "Let me get you that summer blanket," she says, "it's chilly tonight. Come on, I think it's in the linen closet, we'll put that on the bed and you'll be warm as toast."

It's the dark that worries them, I think as I lie in my bed under the summer blanket that smells of moth-

balls. In the daytime they don't care if we're alone together but in the dark they conjure wickedness. The
dark hides and erases, shades the desiring of their secret selves.

My journal says:

> A Nothing Day
> The moon is going, soon it will be gone. I no
> longer know who my parents are. If they look
> for their daughter they will not find her. She has
> become the child of the nightcatcher. She has
> become part of him.

EIGHT

Life is such a precarious thing, change the angles of
words and thoughts and the slipping kaleidoscope al-
ters its pattern. Like pieces of colored glass, our day
takes form. Aunt Ev's towers and raspberries, like
black rods, brown triangles, rose-colored circles on a
sea of green.

"I'm going down to get that muffler," Uncle Tim
says after breakfast. "You kids want to come along?"

"Oh Tim, it's such a nice day . . . they don't want to
sit in a garage."

And somehow we decide, in early morning kitchen
conversation, to walk to the tower.

"You know," Aunt Ev says, "if you wanted to pick
some raspberries, I could maybe make a tart for dinner . . . that is if the birds haven't got them all."

"Take the basket," Uncle Tim suggests. Aunt Ev
has to get down on her hands and knees and search in
the bottom cupboard, complaining, "Where did I put
that thing, I haven't seen it in years."

The basket, big and old, has to be dusted, and sits
on the kitchen table, empty, tempting, and Aunt Ev
decides to pack a picnic lunch. "After you eat it, you
can fill it up with the raspberries."

"They'll never get that much," Uncle Tim laughs.

The basket gets filled up with things you can't imagine. Chicken and fruit salad and deviled eggs. I think of my picnics at home, tuna fish sandwiches and egg salad. Nothing as exotic as wine glasses for lemonade. Aunt Ev puts in linen napkins instead of paper ones. "Bring those back," she says. I catch Uncle Tim looking at me in a peculiar way. What's showing on my face, I think, what does he see that I don't know myself?

We go forth like characters in a fairy tale. Bradley shakes his head, laughing. "Too much," he says.

"Do you want some bug repellant?" Aunt Ev calls after us. "Don't get poison ivy!"

"They really seem very nice, Bradley. But I can't help waiting for it to end. Do you think they're actually going to let us go to New Life?"

"No thinking today," Bradley says, "just smelling, breathing, walking." His long taut leg moves next to mine as we go up the hill. "I hope I remember how to get there."

The trees are full of music, the sunlight is dancing. I feel the way I haven't felt in weeks and I get the old goblin pain back again, filling me with excitement. Only in the momentary shadows do I remember Sugar Creek. No thinking today. No remembering.

But you can't really stop your mind from thinking. You can't keep your mouth from talking. We end up remembering anyway. Yet somehow in the middle of the woods it seems farther away than ever before. It's like we're discussing some book or a movie. Other planets, other times, things that happened in a different life. The forest begins to enchant us.

Up and up we go, the basket between us. Greenness closing in. When we stop to rest it's so quiet I begin to feel like faces are watching me, peering out from behind tree trunks, silent mirth from under leaves. Spirits with wings, souls in wood.

"Do you know what this reminds me of?" Bradley whispers.

"No what?"

"An Ingmar Bergman movie." He looks over his shoulder. The spell is cast on him too. "I expect a dark coach to come through the trees, The Magician will smile at us, the virgin on the white horse will thunder past, chased by demons, and we'll all dance, holding hands, to the top of the tower."

"Bradley! You have them all mixed up."

"I know, dopey."

"You're scaring me."

"Don't be scared, Apple. This is where the peace is. This is where we can lie down and hear the earth's turning." He puts his fingers to his lips. "Ssssh, listen. The forest is alive. And we're the only humans in it."

When we reach the legs of the tower it's like being jolted out of a dream. An unexpected man-made thing looming up through the dense underbrush. Vines are growing through the cracks in the wooden stairs. The stairs go around like the inside of a lighthouse and we go upward, like climbing to heaven. Out of the pale green shadows and into hot sunlight.

It's like looking out over the whole world. Miles and miles of green hills. You can't see a road or a car or a house at all. There's nobody alive down there except maybe Indians. I wonder why humans are needed at all. The earth is fulfilling itself without us. It's been here so long, it must go on longer. It almost makes me believe in the continuity of time and life. Something I haven't felt before, something that makes me unafraid. An unbelievable peace settles down on me. I never want to go back.

We eat our lunch up there, getting roasted in the sun. And the heat, a reminder of other suns, brings to our minds the memory of cool water, an awareness of our bodies slipping through liquid pools. Without speaking we put everything back into the basket, Aunt Ev's linen napkins, the empty glasses, the crumpled wrappings of our food.

We lower ourselves down into the sea of grass, like divers without enough oxygen, it takes our breath away. Our clothed bodies touching nearer than we could have imagined before, we sink into the water-less pool, rippling the vines, disturbing last autumn's leaves.

"Do you want to?" he asks me.

"I don't know." And I really don't. Because the view from the tower has renewed me, made me feel that I don't need everything so fast anymore, that we can take our time and love each other slowly, as slowly as Bradley turns toward me and kisses me, leaning his body gently on me, and something happening but not everything not completely. We lie very quietly, waiting for our hearts to stop pounding, waiting for our lungs to fill with whispers again, waiting to find the earth's slow turning again.

It's getting late. We better go pick the raspberries. Reluctant to leave, to stand up and become two people again. He finds me a four-leaf clover. Puts it through the buttonhole of my shirt.

But I do not need a souvenir of you, no trinket could recall your form. You are the sea, the air, the forest floor, the life that breathes in my own mouth.

"You're late," Aunt Ev says. "I was getting worried."

We rush to the door, overly breathless, too loud and talkative about our find of raspberries. My voice soars, "The birds didn't get them all!" Spilled raspberries turning the sink red and purple. Aunt Ev moves through our joy in silence. Does it show? Do we move together in some new way? I know we avoid looking at each other all of a sudden. I know I pull my hand away from Bradley's accidental touch.

Lying alone in my bed. Listening to the humming stars, spilled starlight, splashed nighttime. I did go walking to the brink of myself. I am almost a woman now. The next time I will be. Wind etched in leaves. The dark is like someone quiet and smooth lying next to me.

In the morning Bradley has a big argument with Uncle Tim. He tells him we're going to New Life. I go outside and sit on the sawed-off tree stump but I can still hear them arguing. Aunt Ev moves around in the kitchen, her lips clamped shut, not saying a word. I guess they're both hurt and disappointed. But although I feel sorry for them, I can't see how they really expected us to stay. I guess they thought everything was fine, that we had satisfied our running-away syndrome, that all we wanted was a change of address for a while and then we'd go back and take up where we left off. I suppose that's what they told Bradley's parents. They were planning to be our chaperones and everybody was going to be happy as pie. I knew it all along. Nobody could be that sugar sweet. It was all a big act and now they're going to show their true colors. The minute we leave they'll call the police and the National Guard. I wish Bradley hadn't told them. We should have just taken off.

"Alex, would you come in here please," Aunt Ev calls.

My feet feel like lead. I slouch into the kitchen, prepared for the worst. "In the living room," Aunt Ev says. That's worse than worse. It sounds too formal. We'll have to sit straight in our chairs with our hands folded waiting for the axe to fall.

Bradley is sitting on the edge of the couch. Uncle Tim is sitting on the edge of the coffee table, facing Bradley, his hands clamped between his knees. His face is red and his eyes look hurt. But I can't find any anger. How can he not be angry? "Now, do you want to go along with this?" he asks me.

Aunt Ev flutters behind me. "Sit down, Alex," she says, "sit down."

"Yes," I say. Very clearly. Maybe a little belligerently.

"Okay, okay," Uncle Tim puts his hand up as if to ward off a blow, "and how do you plan to get to this place?"

I look at Bradley. He says, "Hitch. Thumb our way there."

"Oh no you're not," Uncle Tim says and I want to leap up out of my chair and run out the door. "If you're so damned determined to go there, you're not going to do it by thumbing rides. I'm taking you."

Aunt Ev says, "Won't you kids reconsider?"

"Ev," he yells, and now his voice is angry, "what's the use of arguing anymore?" He gets up. "It's settled, it's finished. You get ready." He goes out, like an explosion. We can hear a door slam.

I realize they really are sad we're going. Not only because they don't approve but because they'll miss us. Incredible as it seems, they like us! Not the way parents like you because you're their children, but as people. It could almost make you want to change your mind but we're not falling into any traps like that.

We pack our stuff and Aunt Ev adds about eighteen shopping bags full of "supplies" to take along. She thinks we're going to starve to death and get eaten by tigers.

My life is becoming a series of good-byes. Fade-outs in a film, the music swelling and everybody getting up out of their seats and going home. Only Bradley and I stay on the celluloid, we keep on traveling long after the lights are on and the background music has stopped playing. Aunt Ev waves us off. Good-bye again.

I still don't trust Uncle Tim. I keep watching the road, expecting him to be taking us back to Ravanna River.

Boy are you jaded, I tell myself.

"What are you smiling about," Uncle Tim asks me, and he smiles back.

I turn around and look at Bradley. He's smiling too.

NINE

We turn left at the Dairy Queen and drive down a bumpy dirt road and suddenly New Life sprawls in front of us.

A bunch of brown buildings, some of them like old shacks, a couple of tents huddled together, a half-finished brick wall. There are long clotheslines strung from trees and poles and all kinds of clothes are hanging out to dry: sheets, blue jeans, socks, smocks, long skirts, baby clothes. On the side of the nearest house, "Hare Hare" is painted in large, drippy red letters.

A bunch of chickens squawk and run as the station wagon swings into the yard. There's a girl standing on a bucket, precariously balancing, waving her arms in the air. Uncle Tim leans out and asks, "This New Life?"

The girl gets off the bucket and comes slowly toward the car. She doesn't look too enthusiastic about seeing us. "This is called Deliverance now," she says.

Uncle Tim turns to Bradley in the back seat, "This where you want to be?"

"Yes," Bradley says, already getting out the back door, "yeah, it's okay." To the girl he asks, "Is John Baker here?"

"Oh yea, John," she answers.

"Is he around?"

"I'll show you."

"I'll stick around till you make sure about your friend," Uncle Tim offers. But Bradley is moving off with the girl. Her long skirt blows against her legs. "Well," Uncle Tim says to me, "What do you think about this place?"

"It's okay." I don't think anything about it, actually. It looks depressing so far. Unfriendly.

"I hope you and Brad make it okay. You know you

can always count on us. You get into any kind of trouble, we're just a phone call away."

"Yes."

"You remember that now?"

"Yes. Thanks." We sit in silence, the sun beating through the windshield of the car, we watch the chickens come back, pecking cautiously in the dirt.

"Don't expect too much out of life, try to meet it halfway," he says.

"Yes."

"Do you think Brad knows that?"

"I don't think Bradley expects anything," I tell Uncle Tim, getting annoyed with his talking. In a way, I wish we'd come alone. It's like Uncle Tim is dropping us off at some summer camp.

"Bradley expects too much," Uncle Tim says. His voice is even, he's not angry, just resigned. "He considers himself an outsider, some kind of special misfit in society. He *says* he wants to go his own way, do his own thing, what have you. But underneath it all he wants people to agree with him. He wants the reassurance. He thinks he's going to change the world to get it."

"I don't believe that," I say, feeling I must defend Bradley, but not really knowing how. "He just wants to be left alone."

"Honey," Uncle Tim says, smiling sadly, "nobody can be left alone."

I'm relieved to see Bradley coming back. He's with a tall man. The man is dressed in a pair of white shorts and a dazzling white shirt. He's wearing green-tinted teardrop sunglasses and his feet are bare. He looks like a movie producer or somebody ready to play a supersonic game of tennis. He shakes hands with Uncle Tim. "John Baker. How are you, sir?" he says, smiling even white teeth, teeth almost as white as his shirt. He smells of garlic.

Bradley and John Baker get the knapsacks out of the trunk and the rest of the stuff that Aunt Ev and

Uncle Tim have given us. Then there is an awkward moment, when everybody stands around, silent, shuffling feet and squinting against the afternoon sun.

"Well good-bye," Bradley says.

"Good-bye, you two," Uncle Tim says but he seems reluctant to go. "Take care now." He gets back into the station wagon slowly. He reverses gears and backs up, turning the car and dispersing chickens. "Good-bye," he calls again, sticking his hand out and waving, "so long."

I watch the car disappear around the bend. The dust settles. We are really here. "Well," John Baker says in a loud voice, "let me show you how we do things around here."

It seems like now that we're together, Bradley and I are never going to be alone. The men sleep in a dormitory, a couple of the shack-like buildings beyond the garden. The women sleep in their own house, one of the ghastly looking places with turrets and sagging porches and gingerbread trimming all falling to pieces and swinging dangerously in the breeze.

"This used to be a summer resort," John Baker explains. "We're restoring the main buildings, hopefully in time for winter, so we can have central heating. Everybody puts in time for the restoration, as well as doing his own regular job. We have a couple of cats who work as carpenters all the time, you know, but the rest of us do what we can."

He blinks his eyes when he talks, maybe that's why he wears dark glasses. I can see him doing it from the side. It fascinates me. Blink blink blink—we—blink blink—all—blink—share the work.

"Well take a break and groove on the sunset or something," he says. "Take it easy, you won't have a chance from now on." He grins. One of his side teeth is missing but the rest of them are whiter than white. I don't know whether I like him or not. He's a combination of nice (like when he grins) and seedy (like when he gives us the tour and sounds like a high-pressure salesman).

He leaves Bradley and me alone, and we stand in the middle of the dirt yard, staring at our knapsacks and shopping bags and at each other. There's no telling what Bradley is thinking. His eyes reflect the groovy sunset of Deliverance.

The roommate they give me is a girl named Joan. She has a baby who sleeps in an old, dilapidated crib in the corner of our room. It stands up and gurgles at me, its droopy diapers hanging down and looking wet. Its nose is running. "You don't mind the baby?" Joan asks me. "He's no trouble."

Joan says her husband lives in the men's dorm. He's one of the carpenters but he prefers to write songs. "He only writes them down on paper," she explains. "He never sings them. He never plays them. He writes the notes out with a pencil and he erases too much. He sometimes types the words, leaving neat spaces for the notes in between. But before you know it, he's forgotten it's a song and he's filled up ten pages worth and there isn't any room for the music. The songs just keep coming out and filling up the pages."

"Oh," I say to Joan. What else can I say? I don't even know what she's talking about.

Across the hall from us is a room with a big hole in the door where the knob and lock should be. Joan says nobody bothers to lock doors in Deliverance, but Flint, that's her husband, is going to get Mary, that's the woman's name who lives in the room, a new knob and lock. "Sometime," she says, "soon."

Mary has an eight-year-old son named Jesse and she has a problem with her feet. She sits by the window with her feet up on a ten-gallon can. One of Joan's jobs is to take care of Mary.

"But maybe you can like help me now, huh?" she asks me. "I don't have much time with taking care of my own baby and doing the work in the kitchen. Do you know I'm in charge of the kitchen? I have to be because of the baby. I have to be careful. I always listen for the pop when I open the baby-food jars, you know? I mean, it's to tell if there's a vacuum. Otherwise maybe some of them put something in the jar and closed it up again. He can't eat everything, he has a sensitive stomach. So I have to buy that crap in the jar.

"They tell me they're just fooling me, that they wouldn't put nothing in the jar. But you know one time the cat got sick, so I don't trust them. The cat went out on the roof and stuck its legs out stiff and fell over, sailed down to the ground and died. No thanks."

Oh help, something inside of me yells, oh where am I? But I don't say anything. I nod coolly. I pretend it's all in a day's living for me. I pretend I've been there and seen it all before. "Come on," Joan says, "you can help me in the kitchen."

Dinnertime. Joan tells me to ring the bell outside the kitchen door. People start crawling out of nowhere, coming toward the house. The kitchen is downstairs in the girls' dormitory. It has a big old gas stove with six burners and a gigantic oven that doesn't work. Everybody's been trying to repair the oven because since it conked out they haven't been able to bake any bread. Nobody considers buying bread in a store. Joan tells me she's going to give me the recipe for her Cornell bread. She's going to teach me how to make it. If it's all right with everybody else, Joan is going to let me work in the kitchen with her and Hanni, another girl. Hanni has very long matted hair. She keeps brushing it aside as she stir-fries the vegetables for dinner. The ends of her hair shine with the grease from frying.

I'm a victim, I think as I sit down at the long table to eat dinner, I'm a victim of circumstances, a child of my time. I ate wholemeal muffins on sterilized plates. I allowed my mother to poison me with crap in jars and store-bought bread for my peanut butter sandwiches. I believed in Ajax and Clorox and washing machines. I think I'm going to gag.

But, surprisingly, the vegetables are delicious. I forget all about Hanni's hair and start eating. I'm starved.

Bradley winks at me across the table. He says, "Pass the rice, Apple," I suddenly feel glad I'm here. I feel as if I belong.

Later on, I unpack my knapsack and put my meager possessions away in the empty drawer Joan gives to me. There's no dresser, only three drawers lined up against the wall. One is Joan's. One is the baby's. One is mine. I consider writing in my journal but decide against it. I don't want Joan to ask any questions. I tuck it in under my extra underwear and hope nobody will find it.

My bed is a mattress on the floor. It's lumpy, and gives off a faint aroma of urine. Joan has given me a clean sheet. I use my sweater for a pillow. "If Joan doesn't mind, why should I?" I think.

The baby makes little whines in its crib. Joan blows out the candle, the darkness envelops us. I hear her sigh. I hear her scratching her skin. I have a momentary panic, thinking about bugs and lice. So what, so what, I say, everything's relative. Somehow getting lice here is not as bad as getting lice in Ravanna River.

After a while, when I think I've been sleeping, I hear Joan move. She gets up and goes out the door. She doesn't come back until morning.

TEN

Deliver us from our days at Deliverance. Sometimes that's the way I feel. But most times, I like it. I believe we're all working together for something worthwhile.

Since I've been here I haven't:

1. Been alone with Bradley (except for once in a while).
2. Taken a bath.
3. Read a book.
4. Called my mother.
5. Been alone with Bradley.

It's very puritanical here, my mother would like it.

Maybe I should call and tell her. But she wouldn't believe me. She thinks all communes are promiscuous. She'd never believe that Bradley hasn't even kissed me! Not that kissing isn't allowed, it's just that we never seem to get together long enough in the right place at the right time. John Baker has instituted what he calls an "honor system," and that's why the men and women are split up into separate buildings. It's because they've been having all kinds of trouble with the Department of Health and the police and the town nearby trying to make them move. That's why he always wears such blinding white clothes and keeps his hair short. He has to go see people to talk them into letting the community stay. He says if we really believe in what we're doing then we should be able to put personal relationships aside for a while and become one total being, a kind of gestalt.

But I know Joan sneaks out at night to meet Flint. I don't say anything. Even though it's certainly undermining the honor system and not being very honest. But when I see her working so hard in the kitchen, and being kind to everyone, helping them with everything even when she's tired and has circles under her eyes, I can't blame her. Joan does the work of about ten people. So I make a special effort to help her with her baby, taking care of him and taking him outside to play. I really like little kids so I don't mind. He runs around in the yard and chases the chickens and keeps falling down and getting filthy. Before dinner I give him a bath outside with the hose. That's really the only way to get a bath around here which is one of the reasons I haven't taken one yet.

I washed my hair in the laundry sink in the basement of the house. There's no hot water and I had to grit my teeth and do it in cold because if there's anything I can't stand it's dirty hair. I thought I was going to freeze to death or get eaten by rats or who knows. The basement is gloomy and damp and full of spooky little rooms with nothing in them. The pipes all have big growths that look like mushrooms and they drip, making sounds like someone's walking around in the corners. But it was worth it to have clean hair. I sat out in the sun and brushed it dry. It smelled good, too, even though I had to use a cake of soap instead of shampoo. Me, who used to get hysterical if I ran out of creme rinse! If I learn anything here, it will be how to get along without all the materialistic accouterments of life. I remember my medicine cabinet at home and I wonder why I ever needed all that stuff! I used to get worried about getting pimples and I'd use all these special soaps and lotions to prevent them. Around here nobody cares if you have a pimple. And anyway, if you eat the right foods, Joan and Hanni say, you won't get them. I keep checking and waiting to break out and I'm still amazed that I can live without pimple lotion.

We do our laundry outside in a big tub with water from the hose. My underwear looks a little gray but it's clean. It hangs out in the fresh air and smells like Aunt Ev's sheets. Except yesterday my shirt smelled of smoke and burned cornhusks because we made a big fire to roast corn.

We all ate outside last night, roasted corn, and chicken for anyone who eats meat. About half the population here are vegetarians. Then we had a meeting and it was decided that I could be a permanent kitchen helper. Bradley's been doing painting, working on the restoration. "But we have to cop more paint, man," somebody said.

They have these meetings all the time where people get up and say what they feel, or tell what's been annoying them, or ask for suggestions to solve their problems. Everybody listens to everybody else, no matter how long it takes. It's part of being a gestalt society.

Joan got up and told about Mary's feet and said she thought maybe we should get a doctor. Everybody voted against a doctor.

"But she really is sick," Joan said, and you could tell

that Joan was feeling all of Mary's pain and discomfort. Then there was a big discussion about vitamins and what to feed Mary and what to soak her feet in. And Joan said, "But suppose she dies," and Flint jumped up and yelled, "Nobody dies here, not on this land. Everybody lives!"

The trouble is that nobody asked Mary for her opinion. Nobody wanted to hear what she had to say about her own feet. I guess if you want to become a real living part of Deliverance, your feet are everybody else's feet too. Mary was upstairs in her room where she always is. But Jesse was down with us. He runs around and can't sit still. Joan says it's because he needs a lot of attention and love and we all have to work very hard to give him all our love. "Just keep on loving him," she says. But sometimes I don't feel like loving Jesse much. He gets on my nerves.

The other day I was sitting with Mary, trying to keep her from getting lonely, and Jesse came in and threw himself down on the bare floor and started rolling around, his knees and elbows hitting and making soft thuds.

"Stop that," Mary said, and I felt like kicking him because his body looked all wrong, mixed up there on the floor. Then he stopped and just stared at the ceiling. His eyes are deep inside him, ancient old eyes in his eight-year-old face. "My feet are killing me," Mary said. "Maybe I should put some ice on them."

Downstairs in the refrigerator there's a big block of ice to keep the milk and butter and meat cool. John Baker goes into the nearest town to buy the ice. We have no electricity here. They came and turned it off because nobody paid the bills. Now John makes sure that the gas bill is always paid. The gas comes in big cylinders and is hooked up outside the kitchen window. But the electric company won't turn the electricity back on. They want a big deposit and payment in advance. One of John Baker's jobs is trying to convince them to reconnect. When he goes to see them he wears what he calls his P.R. suit.

I don't know what to do about Mary's feet. I don't even like to look at those feet! Sometimes dark blood oozes out of her toes, growing bright, brighter, looking like red paint. She gets Jesse to wrap them up in a piece of old toweling. She sits all day by the window, sometimes singing. "Where he runs . . ." she sings, "in my mind . . . where I live in joy." Hanni told me that Mary had a doctorate in music. I look at her and I wonder how it feels to be her. And then I think, I am her. I'm Alexandra, and Mary, and Joan and everybody else.

Mary showed me a snapshot of herself when she was a child. She had a little round head and she was smiling at the camera, and behind her was her mother telling her to say Cheese! and her aunt and her cousin, Inette. She looked like she didn't have a thing to worry about, that nothing was ever going to happen to her.

Before I came here, I never knew people like Mary and Jesse and Joan existed. All I knew was Ravanna River where everybody goes to the doctor for the slightest little problem. I can't imagine anybody in Ravanna River sitting with their feet up on an old can, mopping up the blood with a towel. The trouble is, I still don't know which is right. I still sort of believe in doctors and medicine and being taken care of properly. And I hope I never get sick here. I'm afraid of them having a meeting and deciding not to call a doctor for me. I guess I'm afraid of dying.

I think of death mostly at night. I think how you won't remember who you are anymore. It's no comfort to believe in heaven and life in the hereafter as my Sunday-school teacher used to say. Even if there is such a thing, it won't be the same as now. I mean, I won't be Alexandra Appleton, with an address and phone number and preferences in food and clothes. I won't have a body or a stomach or a name. They don't give you the facts in Sunday school. They let you imagine heaven as just another place to live. They don't tell you the truth because they don't know it themselves. When you're little, you can believe in it without considering practicalities. But when you're older, it all begins to seem kind of funny. Then you start really thinking: What is it really like to die?

Most of the time I take the easy way out: I don't think about it. I get up in the morning and help Joan change the baby, and I take the dirty diapers down and wash them. I set the table for breakfast and make coffee and boil water for anyone who wants tea. We have oatmeal and Granola and fruit for breakfast. Eggs are for lunch because they're cheap. They get eggs from the chickens here but sometimes have to buy more. Somebody drives to a farm where they sell organic eggs.

The only thing anybody ever argues about is money. There's no bread for a doctor, they say, and no bread for eggs, and they all hate the idea of needing so much money to survive. Sometimes they talk about getting a grant from a big company or a university and sometimes they get bitter and say they'll just rip off the establishment. I keep thinking about how my mother used to write out a check at the supermarket, sometimes for forty or fifty dollars, and how I used to ask her to buy me stuff at the health-food store.

"But it's so expensive, Sandy," she'd say.

"It's worth it, Mom," I'd tell her. I always assumed the money was available. I never considered having to do without it.

The things I dread most are a car driving up and when we get mail. The mail comes to a post-office box and people get letters from friends who used to live here or friends in Amsterdam or even their parents. Sometimes they get money which they immediately put into the fund, just the way Bradley and I put most of our money in when we came here. Nobody thinks about keeping money to themselves and I feel a little guilty because I didn't donate all of mine. But I kept thinking I had to save some for an emergency. My mother's voice got in my brain and kept telling me, "Save some for a rainy day." It's hard to undo your past.

Bradley sent his parents a postcard and gave them the box number and I decided I better write one to my parents too. I sent them a picture of a lot of trees and a big lake. On the other side it said Eaglehead Dam, but it didn't give the town. Now I'm sorry I did it and I keep expecting my parents to drive up. Not that they couldn't have found out where I am from Aunt Ev and Uncle Tim anyway. They're nice and all but I can't really see them lying about where we are. I tried to make Deliverance sound like a very well-supervised camp-type place. As I wrote it I kept thinking and wondering if I was lying. Sometimes I think you can't live without lying.

So whenever a car drives up, and if it's not the old battered blue Chevrolet that John Baker owns, or Hanni's Volkswagen or Link Elliott's car, I get scared. Here they come, I think, now it's all over. I don't even stop to consider that my parents don't own the kind of car that's arriving. I just get a case of instant panic.

All kinds of people come around. They get out of the car and stare and ask questions. They act as if we're some kind of animals on display. You can see them thinking how deranged and decadent we must be. I hate them because they remind me of Ravanna River and Total Misunderstanding. Get out of here, I want to scream, Go home and look in the mirror! Bradley says, "It's not worth it," and he just keeps on painting a wall.

Joan talks to them. She tries to make them understand. "If you don't give them love you might just as well be them," she says.

I overheard one man saying, "They're all high on drugs," as he went back to his car, his camera bouncing on his chest. But John Baker insists on Deliverance being clean. We can't afford it now, he says, and he kicked two people out for having drugs just before we came.

There are no drugs here, I feel tempted to write to mother. But that's as good as telling her to come and get me. She'll believe just the opposite is true.

Bradley's father tried to get Ravanna River to hold a series of workshops on drugs. He printed up hand-bills and invited all the parents to come. But hardly anyone showed up. My father was away on business and my mother said she wanted to go but she had too many things to do. Bradley told me his father talked to the principal of the junior high school to try to convince him to have the same program on drugs that the high school did. The principal said he didn't believe in stirring everything up. The more you talked about those things, he said, the more trouble you have. Bradley's father called him an ostrich. That's one of the reasons I liked Bradley's parents better than my own.

I don't know whether smoking grass is right or wrong. I never tried. Bradley did. He said he liked flying on his own mind better. That's another reason why some of the kids didn't like him in school. He didn't fit in with any particular group. They couldn't figure him out.

I guess I agree with Bradley actually. He says he can get high on life, on writing his books and poetry, on breathing the air in the mountains when he goes camping. Some of my girl friends said I was scared to try. Maybe I was. I was scared of a lot of things but I'm changing. I hope I'm learning to take what life brings by the minute. Without preconceived notions, without automatic reactions. Bradley says you have to do it by the second, you have to clear your mind. I hope we're getting our minds cleared in Deliverance. Otherwise, we'd just be running away in circles.

I guess the only thing I don't like here is not being with Bradley all the time. For the first time in my life I feel jealous. But of what? Of everybody else wanting

Bradley to be part of them. Then I look at him standing out in the hot sun, sweat pouring down his face
and bare back, paint running all over his hand and
arm, and he looks happy and I think I'm being child-
ish. We have all the time in the world, I tell myself,
don't try to gobble the minutes up all at once.

I write in my journal: You are the centaur. The
one that dances on the hill that is my heart

ELEVEN

Days bleed into one another. I wash so many dishes I'm
getting dishpan hands. People around all the time, it's
hard to think a private thought. I see Bradley in the
morning, washing with the hose. He puts his whole head
under the stream of water and when he stands up his
wet hair runs rivulets down his back, wetting the waist-
band of his jeans.

He isn't feeling happy. Somebody stole a whole
stack of his manuscripts, took them out of his knapsack. At dinner time he got up and said that he didn't
mind if somebody wanted to read what he had written, he just hoped they would put the papers back
again when they were finished. He wasn't going to ask
questions, he just wanted the stuff back. But so far,
nothing has turned up.

He laughs in a lopsided, half-sad way. "I shouldn't
be so surprised," he says. "I can't expect the people
here to be any different from people anywhere else."

Maybe it's stupid but I have to say, "But I thought
they were, I thought we were all working together, un-
derstanding each other."

"Let's say they're trying," he says. "They're trying
very hard." He wipes the water out of his eyes. "Just
words, just thoughts, I have more inside."

It's not that he cares if they read his private

thoughts. He's not afraid of that, the way I am of somebody reading my journal. But it hurts him to think that someone would steal. And it makes me start thinking. What else is going to happen?

No sooner do I ask that question than life comes up with the answer. Hanni comes back with the mail. She hands Bradley a letter. My heart thuds, afraid she's going to hand me an envelope too. Bradley is staring at the address, as if he's forgotten how to read his own name. "Who's it from," I ask, hoping he'll say Uncle Tim, Aunt Ev, but he doesn't answer. He shoves the envelope into his pocket and starts winding up the hose.

Joan calls me from the doorway, "Allllll, here's Bumps for you!" Bumps is a dumb nickname she gave her baby because he falls down so much. I always call him Jimmy which is his rightful name. I take the baby from her and turn, holding him in my arms, looking for Bradley. The sun is in my eyes. He's walking away. Hanni asks, "Did you peel those vegetables yet?" Bobbie, a girl who works in the garden, comes over and starts talking to Jimmy, making him giggle by tickling him under the chin. I'm surrounded by people and Bradley is disappearing, taking the letter away, leaving me with nervous questions, a pounding heart, all kinds of dread.

I suddenly feel like I can't stand another minute in Deliverance. If I don't get away from people I'm going to scream. But I just stand there, holding Jimmy, smiling at Bobbie, as if nothing is bothering me. Joan and Hanni and Bobbie start talking about food, and the weather and what should they have for lunch and it's as if they're babbling nonsense, another language. I put Jimmy down and take his hand and very slowly we walk away. Jimmy gurgles and laughs and if it wasn't for my holding him up, he'd get down and crawl around in the dirt. "Come on, little boy," I tell him, "come on."

I take him over near the clothesline where he can

play in the grass. I sit down in the shade of somebody's green-striped sheets. My stomach feels the way
it used to when I had an exam, excited and sick. I
feel strange. What am I doing here anyway? And I
try to think of myself living in Deliverance for the rest
of my life, growing old, finally dying. It's too frightening a thought. I can't stay here forever. Even if I
believe in this way of life, a community of peace and
love and organic vegetables and everything, I can't
imagine spending my whole life surrounded by all
these people. And then I realize that every time I
started thinking that way, I squelched it. Every time I
had a doubt, I tried to hide it from myself.

Maybe I just want to go home.

"Don't get yourself all worked up about nothing,"
I hear my mother's voice saying. When I used to
worry and worry about whether I'd pass my science
test, or whether I'd get on the swimming team, or
whether I had some horrible disease, my mother would
tell me to stop thinking about it. "Worry about it when
it happens," she'd say, "not before." And she'd take
me to the doctor and I wouldn't have the horrible
disease; or I'd get an 85 on the science test, or I
wouldn't make the swimming team and was happy
I didn't. Then I'd wallow in the relief and promise myself that the next time I wouldn't get myself "all
worked up."

But you never learn your lesson. The next time you
do exactly the same thing, spend days and nights worrying again.

I try anyway. I tell myself it's ridiculous to worry
about what's in Bradley's letter. So what if it's from
his parents, it doesn't necessarily mean bad news. I
try to weave a spell out of my mother's advice. If I
don't waste time worrying, then it will turn out all
right. It's going to be okay anyway, so don't bother
thinking about it.

The morning takes a million years to be over. Jimmy eats a big glob of dirt and grass and I get angry

and yell at him. Then I'm sorry. I take him back to
the kitchen and wash his hands and face and put him
in the highchair that Joan got at the Salvation Army
and I give him an oatmeal cookie. He's already forgotten that I yelled. He smiles at me.

I have to wait until the afternoon. After lunch, and
dishes and putting things away, Bradley and I can
take a walk. Please don't let anything happen to prevent the walk, I pray to nobody in particular. And
please let us be alone. But Bradley doesn't come for
lunch. I wait and wait and hope he'll show up but by
the time everybody has eaten and the dishes are
waiting to be washed, I give up. I start stacking the
dirty plates and carrying them to the sink. Meals are
very organized here. Joan told me that when she first
came everybody ate at any old time and whoever
wanted to cook just started cooking. It was very cha-
otic and people kept having arguments over who
cleaned up and who didn't, so Joan took over the
kitchen and all the meals. There's no way I can get
out of washing the dishes. It has to be done. I feel like
my mother, slaving away in the kitchen, saying, "It
has to be done, Sandy, it has to be done." My mother
always hates to clean up after a party. She says, "This
damn dishwasher is too small," and "Look at all
those rings on my table," and I wonder why she ever
gives parties anyway, she spends so much time complaining beforehand about getting all the food ready,
and during the party she's always rushing around getting people things and emptying ashtrays. Afterwards she
says to my father, "That's the last party I'll ever give
for those people." It's like dirty dishes follow you
around for your whole life, you can't escape from
them.

But at least I can be alone in the kitchen. Joan
takes the baby upstairs for his nap. Hanni goes out to
lie in the sun and everybody else disappears, not wanting to be around to have to help. So I stand at the sink
and pretend it's my kitchen, and Bradley is outside

working on our land and maybe we have a baby upstairs taking a nap. The sun comes in through the window and shines on the damp silverware. The plates
clink together. My thoughts stop racing through my
head. I feel calm for about five minutes until I start
thinking about finding Bradley and asking him about
the letter.

As I cross the yard and walk toward the restoration,
I feel myself getting anxious. I can hardly wait to run
up the stairs to where Bradley's been working. The
place smells of paint fumes and the stairs creak. The
room he's been painting white is empty. A big paint-
brush is soaking in a can of turpentine. My shoes
scuff up the newspaper that's all over the floor. Downstairs again. Outside. I find him on the side of the
house, talking to Link Elliott.

Link Elliott is one of the people I don't like very
much here. He drinks Mountain Berry wine out of the
bottle even though most people in Deliverance don't
believe in drinking alcohol. John Baker is always
telling him to get rid of his damn wine bottles and Link
says, "What are you scared of, boy, liquor is legal."

When Link sees me coming he waves his hand and
takes off. I guess maybe he knows I don't like him.

"Hi," Bradley says.

"Hi." Suddenly I'm tongue-tied.

"Come on let's take a walk." He takes my hand
and we start walking. He's very quiet. I can tell he's
thinking. When he thinks very hard he forgets who
he's with. But now he's thinking about problems, not
his books or his poetry, the way he used to do when
we took walks in Ravanna River. We could walk for
hours without saying anything at all. Then suddenly
he would say, "How's this . . . ?" and rattle off a poem
or give me a plot. I feel sad now. I feel like we ought
to be back in Ravanna, walking around the reservoir with nothing to worry about.

Finally I have to ask him, "Bradley, do you want to
tell me about the letter?"

He shakes his head no. "Not yet, at least. Let's talk about something else first."

But neither one of us can think of anything to talk about. We're both thinking about the letter and now I know it isn't going to be "nothing to worry about, no problem." Then he stops and takes it out of his pocket. He doesn't want to show it to me, he thinks he shouldn't, but "No secrets, remember?" and he hands it to me. "No secrets," he says.

Words on paper becoming the person, Bradley's mother, sitting in the kitchen in her blue robe, holding a cigarette and a cup of coffee, words becoming the hurt inside, thin spidery blue marks that match the blue robe.

Dear Bradley, I feel that now you've taken this drastic step to become an independent adult, albeit prematurely, I must say . . .

Words winding themselves around heart and mind, tightening the web that keeps a child a child.

I must say that you shouldn't, you mustn't

(deep blue underlines to nail the lid),

you mustn't throw your life away for the sake of one mistake with a girl. These things happen, we all know that, and we're not blaming you, but we feel you are going too far in doing what you think is right. There is no need to let your life be wasted, with all your potential you need your education. Something like this must not be allowed to alter our plans, your plans for the future.

The web is spun, the sun glistens on the innocent trap, so fragile, so deadly.

Running off is not the answer, you'll only regret

it in the end. And I hope I can speak freely, Bradley dear, and tell you that marriage is not the answer either, we would not force you to marry her. Since we are discussing this as adults, I must say that things can be arranged to everyone's benefit, and that there are certain steps that can be taken providing you and Alexandra return home in time.

The letter sends all its love, for love of Bradley, the blue curves closing in well-meaning ignorance.

"Bradley, they think we ran away because I'm pregnant," and I start to laugh, laughing long, falling down on the grass and putting my nose against its realness because nothing else can be real now. They blame me.

"Apple, get up," and Bradley puts his arms around me. I realize I'm not laughing, I'm crying.

"They think it's all my fault."

"Nothing's your fault," Bradley says.

But it is, Bradley. I never should have come with you, you should have gone alone. I've only made things worse for you, I've messed things up. It was wrong and selfish, I realize now. I only came because I didn't want to let you go.

You can't capture love and lock it up. If you really love someone, you set them free. I've only done what our parents want to do, put the heart in chains and hold it close, so afraid of losing it to life.

"I'm the one who should go home, not you."

Bradley is silent, and in his silence I am already gone, giving his life back to him to live.

"No," he says, "don't go back for me." His face is angry. "I'd like you to stay with me. I'm not going back there."

I turn over on my back and look into the sun. Blinding light that burns my tears. What should I do?

"Do you want to go home?"

"No," I whisper.

And I put myself back into the muddle. Making a decision that is no decision at all.

Deep deep sleep. It's like coming up out of a pipe in the basement. Racing up the perpendicular tunnel of night, up I go, as slow as thick molasses, my mouth and eyes stuck shut, only my ears can hear.

I wake up, not wanting to, not wanting to remember anything. Someone is crying. I look over to the next mattress to see if it's Joan. The mattress is empty. The baby is in his crib, curled up at the end, sleeping quietly.

Mary. Mary must be crying across the hall. I lie there and listen to the sound of it, more frightening than in the daylight. I don't want to know. I hope it will go away. If I close my eyes I can slip back into sleep, forget the crying, forget everything again.

But it goes on, getting louder. The baby turns over, makes a little sighing sound. He'll wake up. I have to get up and see what's the matter. Do things for other people, Bobbie and Hanni and Joan say, things that you might not want to do, but things that will help them, make them happy. Lose yourself and become everyone else.

I get up and go to the door, sort of crawling my way there, almost afraid to stand up. Hunched over, I go into the hall, shivering even though it's stuffy and hot in the house. It's so dark, only the flickering shadows on the far wall, made by the little candle-warmer that sits in a dish at the top of the stairs so we won't kill ourselves if we have to go to the bathroom in the middle of the night. The sound of crying comes through the half-opened door to Mary's room. I push it all the way open with a shaking hand. Peer in. Mary is in the corner, huddled near a single candle. A book is lying beside her. And a half-finished bottle of Coke. There's a puddle under her bare feet. A funny smell in the room.

Then a scratching behind me and Jesse appears, scaring me to death. Jesse, Jesse your mother's sick, run and do something right for a change, run and get a doctor. Jesse stands there, his eyes daring me to stop his mother's crying.

I run out into the hall and run up and down like a crazy woman, forgetting to knock on any of the doors. "Where's Joan, get Joan," I say, "get Joan!"

Somebody says, "What's the matter?" Candle faces appear, looking like skulls, figures in a dream unrecognizable. They don't understand me.

"What's wrong with her?" someone else asks.

"Joan," is all I can say.

"Hey Jooooooooooooooooonnnnn," a voice screams out a window.

Joan comes running up the stairs, she's holding her long skirt up over her knees. When she gets to the top she lets it go and it brushes the candle dish and knocks it over. The light goes out. "God, God," Joan pants and runs into our room.

"The baby," she says, "I thought it was the baby."

I feel like somebody in a bad movie. "It's Mary," I tell her. Then everybody is crowding into Mary's room, giving advice, talking all at once.

"Call an ambulance," they say.

"We don't have any bread for an ambulance."

"Oh, it'll be all right," Joan says. "It's nothing serious. Get out of here, will you?"

Mary says, "That doctor won't come here."

Joan says, "Ssssh, Mary, be quiet now."

"I got John," Hanni yells too loud, coming up the stairs with John Baker following her.

John says, "I'll take her to the hospital."

"I'm not going to any hospital," Mary protests. And she starts crying and screaming and won't let him touch her.

"Link went to call an ambulance," somebody announces, and John Baker leans against the wall. "Oh Christ," he says.

Link must have taken his car to call the ambulance. There's no phone in Deliverance. I guess he's one of those people who always does the wrong thing.

I have to get out of that room. I go and sit on the stairs, hugging my knees.

The downstairs door bangs ferociously and two policemen hurry past me, their faces shining sweat. They chug up the stairs, fat and ungainly, fattened by guns and sticks and ammunition on their hips. Behind them come two men in white, lugging a contraption. I sit on the stairs, thinking about getting up and going back to see what's happening, but then they all come out again. Chug chug, the man in front is pulling a stretcher, chug chug, the man behind is pushing it. In the middle, Mary's lumpy body wobbles, covered with a sheet. Don't forget the blood, I feel like telling them. Mary's eyes roll and she doesn't see me. I follow the stretcher down the stairs and out into the yard. The two men maneuver Mary very well. They push the stretcher into the back of the ambulance like a slab of bacon. The siren begins a long slow whine and the ambulance takes off down the road like a white coach, leaving us standing there listening to its wailing sound. My mouth is open with a frozen good-bye. My heart stops beating.

"We're going to close this joint down," someone says behind me, and I turn and see the policeman's glistening face. He and the other one start asking for everybody's name.

A group crowds around them, arguing, protesting, getting angry. I see Bradley standing near the edge of the yard, alone in the shadows. I walk over to him. Nobody sees me going. Nobody pays attention to us. "Bradley," I say, and realize my whole body is shaking, "I don't want to stay here anymore."

I almost say I want to go home.

Bradley whispers, "Apple," and his breath feels hot against my forehead. "Can you get your stuff?" he asks.

And then I'm racing up the stairs again, thinking, people die all the time, I don't even know Mary. I push everything into my knapsack and roll the leftovers in my sweater. The baby is still sleeping. Its mouth makes a little smile. Good-bye, Baby. Good-bye, Joan. I'm sorry I'm going without saying good-bye.

I go out through the kitchen. Out in front, the policemen are talking to John Baker. I can hear another siren, another police car coming closer.

"Nobody did anything," I say to Bradley. He drags me toward the restoration. "Maybe we shouldn't cop out," I say. "Nobody did anything."

But Bradley is pulling me along and I keep dropping my sweater and things keep falling out of it. "Get in," he says.

And I get in a car. The door slams. We take off through a road I never saw before. The dark trees are growing so close they bang on the windshield. We go around a curve and I fall against Bradley. The driver of the car makes a wild, crowing, shrieking sound. I don't have to look to know it's Link Elliott.

TWELVE

It's raining and the road looks greasy, slippery. There are no other cars, we're alone on the highway and this is the way we like it. About an hour ago we passed a gas station and Link filled the tank up with gas. Since then we've only passed some shanties, a dead orchard. The road is snaking through thick trees, branches dripping like a leaky roof. Bradley and I are slouched in the back seat, our shoulders touching, elbows bumping, but we're not talking to each other. The dead silence smells like stale smoke. Nobody wants to talk to anybody. We're all used up.

We're running away. Running away for a long time now. Not like before, protected and guided by aunts and uncles, looked after by Clorox-bleached John Bakers. This is really running, days and nights of diners and gas stations, bottles of orange drink and tough hamburgers. Slipshod, unhealthy humans, bored with each other's guilt. We don't even care if it's raining or shining, one kind of day is as good as another. Time moves us when we can't move ourselves, forc-

ing us to eat, sleep, wipe our dirty noses on our sleeves.
We have no idea where we're running to.

We swerve and Bradley leans on me. So close, I
smell his smell, feel his long hair touch my cheek. He
rights himself and mutters, "Too fast, man," under his
breath. I don't think Link hears. Link is always driving
too fast. Bradley made him promise not to drink any
wine when he drives. Link promised but he doesn't
always keep promises. I worried about it at first. Then
I got tired of worrying.

I think: I am like a plant, without an opinion. All
my emotions have been diluted. Fast or slow, it's the
same as raining or shining. Bradley and I keep moving down this long macadam dream. When we wake
up, things will be all right again. But I don't know
how long it's going to take to wake up.

Sometimes Bradley is like he used to be. Two hours
ago, for instance, he said, "Drink the rain, Apple, it's
good for you." And we stood like two nuts in the
pouring rain, getting our heads wet, tipping up our
faces and opening our mouths. Now he's gone back
into himself, he's too quiet, too locked up. When he's
like that I don't think he can feel anything at all. He's
like an automaton, his hands and feet programmed to
move and walk. Inside his head is an empty place with
a couple of gears.

I know I should be sensible. I should talk to Bradley and we should plan what we're going to do. But it
seems like I can never get away from Link's presence.
And when I do, Bradley is in a bad mood and doesn't
want to talk. It's too hard to decide all by myself. I
only end up feeling guilty. And I know I shouldn't be
here at all. Bradley is always worrying about me. Am
I eating enough, am I sleeping enough, will I catch
cold? I'm a big pain in the neck to him, I know. Maybe if he was alone, he could do something better. Maybe it's worrying about me that puts him in these bad
moods.

But like the plant I am, I do nothing, make no decisions, I simply exist in the flowerpot of my world. I allow myself to slide back and dwell in dreams, memories of what used to be.

I think a lot about the past. I think of all the things we used to do in Ravanna River, how we used to play together and pretend we were cowboys and Indians. Bradley used to tie me to a tree and that made my mother mad. She was always coming out to make a speech about how dangerous it was to tie people up and how we should try to behave ourselves. Act like a lady, she always told me.

I can think back easily in the dark. Until the trees are no longer visible, until they become unknown massive shapes looming against the windows, big monsters on the glass. The headlights trace the double yellow line on the surface of the slippery road. Link holds the wheel with one hand and reaches in his pocket for a cigarette. He punches the lighter in the dashboard and it pops back, glowing and lethal. The smoke drifts back. Ssscreeech, the tires go around another curve. Link grabs the wheel with both hands again, hunches forward and stares down the road. The cigarette hangs on his lip.

Going back in time, I'm a pale thin girl in a cotton dress that ties in the back with a bow. It's horrible, that bow, it falls limp and flat and nobody else has on a dress that ties with a bow. All the girls in my class seem to be wearing nicer dresses than mine, more grown-up than a stupid old cotton dress with a bow and ruffles in the front. I complain to my mother that I like the other girls' dresses better and my mother says, "Don't be envious, Sandy," but I can't help it, I'm the most envious person in the whole world.

"You look lovely, dear," my mother says, and she turns away and starts talking to a friend of hers and I feel all alone in the middle of the gym even though my whole sixth-grade class is there and all their parents too. We're having a dance at the end of the term, before we go to junior high school. The parents organized the whole thing and decorated the gym with balloons and streamers and flags. Records are playing but nobody is dancing. I don't think anybody wants to be the first one. And besides, they're all the wrong kind of records, the kind of records nobody knows how to dance to anyway. I certainly don't want to dance. I don't even know how. I never actually danced with a boy, just with some girls at their houses. So I just stand there, feeling like dropping right through the floor.

Then I see Bradley. "Hey Bradley," I say and rush over to him. He's trying to hide behind the crepe-paper streamers. His hair is slicked down with gunk, looking like gun-metal fibrosis instead of hair. He's wearing a blue blazer and his tie is choking him to death. He smiles sickly at my approach and looks like he has to go to the bathroom.

"Hey, what are you doing here?" I ask him because he told me he wasn't coming to the dance no matter what.

"She made me," he says. His mother is at the refreshment table. She's holding a cigarette and stirring the punch in a big glass bowl. "What's wrong with your hair?" he asks me. I feel terrible. I forgot about my hair. The night before my mother set it on her rollers, spreading each strand with sticky gel before she wound it up.

"The same as yours," I tell him. And then we start laughing.

Laughing. Bradley and I don't laugh much anymore. Except once in a while like when we were drinking the rain. We used to laugh all the time. But maybe that's not what life's all about. Maybe when you grow up you give up laughing.

We used to play grown-up all the time. We had King and Queen grown-up where we put lampshades on our heads and used fireplace pokers for our scepters. We got in a lot of trouble with Bradley's mother for that. And we played husband and wife grown-up but my mother yelled at us for lying down together in my parents' double bed. "That's enough staying in the house," she said. "Go outside and get some fresh air."

But sometimes Bradley was very serious as a child. He once came to my house and when my mother asked him what he wanted he said, "I'm coming to teach Alex the times table so she won't have to cheat anymore." Because I couldn't remember it and I was always looking at somebody else's paper. And he was serious when he told me all the things he wanted to do in life. He knew he could tell me everything and I would never laugh or make comments like the other kids did. He told me he thought he could never have enough time to do everything he wanted to do. He wanted to live ten lives at once, he wanted to be everything, try everything. He'd get so excited he'd have to jump around and yell and scream. "I love everything," he'd say. "I'm never going to die. I'm going to live to be five hundred and forty years old."

I wonder now if Bradley still loves everything. He hardly touches me. At night we lie on the ground, side by side, like unburied strangers. It's not sex that's so important. It's holding someone and being held.

I hear the tires skidding far away, far away from the running water of Ravanna River. I remember Bradley's hand in my hair, summer hands, the touch lingering like raindrops. I can hear the car skidding and I feel the pull to one side. We are turning around in the middle of the road. And then we're righted again, continuing as if nothing has happened, through the monotonous rain, aligning ourselves with the yellow stripes on the glazed night highway. We move through the forest of our minds, keeping secrets from each other. Bradley's eyes are closed.

"Are you tired?" My voice sounds hollow. He doesn't answer. Maybe he's staring into the future, wishing he didn't have to go there.

I close my eyes and try to sleep. But I hear my

mother's voice in my ears. Something is sizzling on the stove. Lamb chops. And baked potatoes in the oven. My father has come home from work and he's taking his coat off in the hall. And then instead of home, I'm in a diner and everything is cooking at once, smoking, burning, greasy, french fries and horsemeat, is what Bradley said we're living on.

Then. The road looks as if it's turning over on itself. An optical illusion, I tell myself, brought on by horsemeat and french fries and ketchup, mustard, onions, relish, pickles, all the extras you can eat for free. Then.

Long road slipped sideways, world turned upside now someone is screaming and the taste and smell of blood is blooming and I do see in my mind's clouded eye the bloodburst like a never-ending birth of roses. Fierce light heats my eyelids and dances my brain and when I look it is staring at me, smoke blinking, right in front of my face. I wait for it to touch me, burn me, but it changes its mind. It puts its long blazing flames on Bradley's hair and he flowers hot haloes and melts before my eyes. Dissolving illusions, revisions of bone and flesh and Bradley is sliding his memory over my heart like breaking fingers. There's no time to say good-bye to him because he has already gone away, the black blue mouth has swallowed his face and part of me runs and says Hurry Up before it happens to you.

Well I guess I'm dead, I think. But instead of dying I find myself walking. My feet move against the force that has throttled me, my legs push against the momentum of the car. I mumble words that sound like the words of prayers. My skin hurts. The bottom of one foot hurts. When I look down I see that my shoes are gone and the toes on my right foot are bleeding just like Mary's toes. The blood is running on the rain-washed road. Find your shoes, a voice says. Sit down and forget it, another one says. The stems of trees are as black as night but the leaves are brilliant, burning in the firelight. I close my eyes. Traveling very fast across the ocean, I can feel the wind, hear the sound of the waves. Boom, the waves explode and the car blows up and Bradley disappears forever, not even his black bones remain.

Once again, a living part of me says Hurry Up. Nobody is going to find you now.

You can vanish forever.

Part Three

A SPRING THAT FEELS
LIKE AUTUMN

ONE

I have entered a new season. It is my season and I am changed. For one thing, I don't have bad dreams and wake up and scream anymore. Even my mother is finally beginning to relax. The other night, she and my father went out to the movies and left me alone in the house. When they came home, I was already in bed, asleep. I left them a note:

> Dear Mom and Dad—
> Everything was fine. Mrs. Trahey called and said she would call you back tomorrow. Please wake me up at seven because I have a biology test. Love, Sandy

I think Mrs. Trahey called because she wanted to check up on me. But things like that don't bother me anymore. I told her all about what I was watching on television. I think she was pretty bored by the time she hung up.

I've been going to school since last month. It's funny how you think about something for so long, worry about it so much, and then when it's happening you just survive, you find yourself going through the motions, and all your big dreads never come to pass. The Monday morning that I was starting school I was a nervous wreck. I woke up at five A.M. and I couldn't get back to sleep again. I felt like I'd been awake the whole night anyway, everytime I turned over it felt like it should be morning.

I stayed in bed and kept thinking about how it was going to be to walk through those doors and go upstairs to my homeroom. I must have made that journey about a million times in my mind. I knew where I was supposed to go because they sent a postcard in September, telling me my new class and homeroom teacher. Mr. Alvador, the language arts teacher. Everybody thinks he's sexy and I kept wishing I had somebody less conspicuous like Mr. Duncan or Miss Murphy. Finally, I couldn't stand it anymore, I had to get up, five A.M. or not. I opened my closet and looked at all my clothes again. I already had my clothes picked out the night before but I thought maybe I would change my mind. Again. We're not allowed to wear jeans to school but we can wear corduroy or woolen pants. My mother wanted me to wear the brown suit with my new brown shoes. I told her I absolutely refused to be seen in that getup. Do you know who finally said I didn't have to wear it? My father! I couldn't believe it.

He said, "Let Sandy decide what she wants to wear on her first day back." That was that. My mother didn't say another word. I could've kissed him. Of course I didn't. I never kiss my father very much. Oh, I mean, I kiss him hello and good-bye if it's some special occasion but usually we never get very close to one another. I don't know when this no-kissing, no-hugging started between us. When I was a little kid I used to do a lot of things with him and he was always giving me pony rides on his back. And there are pictures in the photograph album of me sitting on his lap and stuff. But not anymore. I used to wonder what the other girls did with their fathers, but it's not exactly the kind of question you want to come out with, like, "Does your father kiss you or not?"

So after he told me I could wear what I liked I felt like kissing him and I was sorry after that I didn't. I should have followed my instincts. It suddenly occurred to me that maybe my father thought I didn't

want him to kiss me! The whole time I've been thinking it was his fault and maybe he had the exact same
problem. So I made a promise to myself that the next
time I felt like giving him a big hug or a kiss I would
do it. It gives me the creeps, actually, it sort of em-
barrasses me but I'm going to force myself.

If I tell Kovalik, she's going to ask, "Why do you
feel that way, Alexandra? Why should kissing your father give you the creeps?" Well, I'll have to psycho-
analyze myself to find the answer to that one. Maybe
the reasons don't even matter anymore. It's like a bad
habit. The longer you stay away from touching someone, the harder it is to ever touch them again.

I feel that way about my mother sometimes. Not
the kissing thing, my mother is always kissing me, but
when she and I have a big argument, the longer I
take to talk to her, or apologize, or make up in some
way, the harder it is to bring myself to do it. After a
while, you're not even mad at each other anymore,
but you still put up this big front.

Anyway, I finally decided on my blue corduroy
pants and my body shirt and a vest. I was just finished
getting dressed when my mother knocked and barged
in. "Sandy, how come you're up already? It's only
quarter to seven."

Ugh, quarter to seven, I had another whole hour before I could even leave for school, and even then I'd
be too early. My father was still in the bathroom so I
had to wait to brush my teeth and wash my face.
And since I usually do all that before getting my
clothes on I felt like the whole morning was upside
down. It feels terrible to be all dressed and have dirty
teeth and an unwashed face. I spent the time getting my books together. Putting in my new pack of
loose-leaf into my binder and sticking some pens in
my suede purse. Then there was nothing to do.

I thought about looking in some of the textbooks but
it was too late for that. I was supposed to have been
doing work in them the whole time I was home. My

mother used to ask me, "Sandy, have you done any of your schoolwork yet?" and I'd always mumble some excuse. I guess she didn't dare put the pressure on since I was considered an unstable character. Oh well, I thought, I'll be way behind in everything and that will give everybody another excuse to talk about me.

You see, I had this big thing about people talking about me. I never even knew I had it until the night before I was going back to school. Suddenly, it seemed to matter that I would be the center of attention. Usually, being the center of attention can be fun, but not now. I had enough of Ravanna River publicity what with being in the nut house. I just sort of wished I could slip back into the groove without anybody noticing. But I guess that would be unrealistic. Well, that's what I was worrying about on Monday morning. I couldn't even eat any breakfast I was so nervous. And the more I thought about it, the angrier I got. I was mad at everybody in school before I even got there!

"Sandy, will you please eat something," my mother started nagging me. I felt like throwing up right on the table. I stuffed a piece of toast in my mouth and couldn't chew it. I had to spit it out in my napkin when they weren't looking. My mother kept saying, "Well," and hopping up and down. My father just sat there eating his breakfast calmly. When he was finished he said, "Good luck, Sandy. Have a good first day." That made my mother nervous because she was busy pretending that the day was no different from any other day, like I'd been going to school since the beginning of the term. I guess she thought it would make me feel better but it only made me feel worse. "Thanks," I said to my father and I thought: should I kiss him now? But I couldn't face it with feeling sick and having to arrange it by getting up from the table, so I just sat there. Then he came over and gave me a squeeze on the shoulder.

" 'Bye."

" 'Bye."

"Good-bye, Frank."

My mother asked me, "Do you want me to drive you to school?"

"No," I said, "I'll walk."

"No thank you."

"No thank you."

It was just like old times. Except my stomach felt like a ton of lead.

So then I walked to school, wishing I'd never get there, or that I was coming home instead of going. I took the long way around the field for two reasons. One, I was still too early. And two, I didn't want to meet Jazz. She told me she was going to wait for me at the south gate and give me moral support. I guess it was mean to let her wait there but I couldn't face her moral support. Feeling like a criminal, I sneaked in the gym door and went upstairs to Mr. Alvador's homeroom. The bell hadn't rung yet. But I didn't have a locker number, so I brought all my stuff into the classroom and picked out a seat way in the back. I prayed it wasn't anybody else's seat. I also prayed that Mr. Alvador wouldn't notice me or else he would ignore me or something. What I couldn't stand the thought of was if he gave some kind of big greeting, like "Welcome back, Alex."

Then somebody came in. It was a girl from my homeroom last year. She sort of looked at me and didn't say anything. She just sat down in the front row and took out a notebook and started writing. Then some more people came in. Somebody said, "Hi, Alex," another person said, "Hey, hi," and a few of them just waved and sat down in their seats. It was like I'd been out sick with a cold or something. When Mr. Alvador came in he shut the door and didn't even look at the back of the room. He sat down at his desk and started calling the roll. If he forgets my name I won't say a word, I thought. But there was only one name ahead of mine. "Jason Allen?"

"Here."

"Alexandra Appleton?"

This froggy voice that I didn't recognize said, "Here." Croak. He didn't even look up. He didn't even act surprised. Nothing.

"George Cox."

"Present."

That's what I mean about surviving. When the bell rang we all got up and started to go out. "Oh Alexandra," Mr. Alaador said, when practically everybody had left.

"Yes?"

"Will you go down to the guidance office and get your schedule?"

"Yes."

"It's nice to have you in my homeroom."

"Thank you." Thank you everybody for being not the way I thought you would be.

Jazz was mad at me, naturally. "Thanks a lot," she said when I saw her outside study hall.

"I'm sorry, Jazz."

"Oh forget it." She went into study hall looking hurt. I followed her, wondering if I should sit next to her. I suddenly didn't know if Jazz and I were going to remain friends. It was like we didn't fit together anymore.

"Alex," a friend of mine whispered, "sit here." I started to sit down and then I stopped. I looked to see what Jazz was doing. She was way at the other end. She was busy whispering behind her hand to somebody else.

I promise I'll talk to her at lunch, I said. But I could feel the bond already broken. We didn't need each other anymore. I had entered a new season . . . the sickness was finally going to be over.

TWO

The telephone rang. It was Owen Andersen. I had finally stopped worrying about him calling. I no longer jumped out of my skin when the phone rang. It was a big relief, and I forgot about it. So, when I least expected it, it was him. My mother answered. "Telephone for you, Sandy," she said. I thought it was probably someone from school.

It was a surprise to hear this voice say, "Hello, is this Alexandra Appleton who plays a mean game of poker?" Well right away I knew who it was and I felt like dropping through the floor.

"Yes it's me," I said, and my voice felt grouchy.

"Where've you been lately?"

"I've been busy." That sounded too mean so I added, "with school." I don't know why I was feeling so grumpy all of a sudden.

"Are you busy on Saturday?"

"When?"

"Saturday."

"I mean, when on Saturday?"

He sort of laughed. I was surprised that it sounded like a nervous laugh. I never thought of Owen Andersen being nervous about anything. "Let's try Friday," he said.

I was talking on the living-room telephone. It has a very long cord on it so my father can drag it around to wherever he feels like sitting. I dragged it out into the hall and hoped my mother wouldn't be able to hear.

"Listen I'll tell you the truth, Owen, I don't think my parents would let me go out with you at night."

"That's cool," he said. "How about the day?"

"Like what?"

"Like anything you want to do."

"I'll have to find out."

"Okay," he said. "Should I call you back?"

"Well, I guess so. Tomorrow."

When I hung up my mother asked, "Who was that, dear?" very casually like she didn't really care but she was dying to know. I had a choice then. I could lie and tell her somebody from my class wanted to ask a question about the homework or I could tell her the truth. But all of a sudden I thought about Sugar Creek and the whole summer, and lying just didn't seem worth it. It really depreciates the value of life. It has nothing to do with the Ten Commandments or hell or whether or not God is real. It just diminishes you as a person. So I said, "It was Owen Andersen."

It took a few seconds for my mother to get it. I guess at first she didn't remember who Owen Andersen was. Then she remembered. "May I ask what that man was doing calling you up on the telephone?"

"He wanted to ask me out."

"He what?"

But I knew that was just a rhetorical question so I kept quiet and waited for the storm to begin.

What's been going on, my mother wanted to know, and how come he called me up in the first place, had I seen him before and did I know how old he was.

"Mom," I said, "calm down," which was the wrong thing to say because she got angry with me for being impertinent and rude and I started screaming that I wasn't a child anymore and what did she think was going to happen if I went out with him.

That's when my father walked in. He must have heard us yelling a mile off because he looked very worried when he came through the front door. "What's the matter," he asked. "What happened?" We both tried to explain at once, and complain at once and my father got annoyed and said, "Let's discuss this calmly."

So my mother told him all the questions she had asked me and then she asked them to me all over again and said I should "explain." My father listened to me without saying a thing. When I was all finished explaining that nothing had been going on, but yes I had been up to the Staneblood place and I didn't know how old he was, my father was quiet for a minute. Then he said, "There's one question that hasn't been answered. Sandy, do you want to go out with him?"

And I remembered excited jealous frightened feelings in the snow, wanting to run and tell someone, Jazz calling, Come Onnnnnn under a dark sky.

My answer was: I don't know, because I can't understand what those feelings mean. Where did they come from? Why does it matter?

My answer was: Yes, because I wanted to be able to do things again, go places without my parents hanging around my neck, be allowed to grow up, stop being Sandy the nut case who might run away any minute, who can't be trusted alone with a boy.

My answer was: No, because it gave me a sick queer feeling in my stomach, made me want to drop the whole subject and never bring it up again, made me want to get rid of the aggravation of Owen and all the decisions. Made me think of Bradley and how Owen was not him . . . My answer was no answer at all.

My father said, "We don't really know him, perhaps if he came over here instead," and I felt depressed. I could just see us sitting in the living room, my mother and father talking about the weather, and Owen Andersen saying, "That's cool." Forget it.

"When he calls I'll tell him I can't go out," I said. My parents looked very surprised. And disappointed. It was like they won the battle and didn't like how it felt to win.

"We'll talk about it some more, Sandy," my mother said. I felt pretty sick of talking. What's the use when nobody really pays attention to what you're saying?

But I never escape from talking. I went to see

Kovalik and I had to talk to her. I told her what happened the day before. I told her how we were going to talk about it again before Owen called.

"And who is this Owen Andersen?" Kovalik asks and I remember that I never told her about him. A little guiltily I say, "Oh he lives up the road," but Kovalik is smart enough not to be satisfied with this lame comment so I have to explain.

And my explaining is like a carefully made web unraveling, the wrong thread pulled and everything coming apart. No longer am I bound up in the secret tapes of time past. One truth leads to another. What I started out to explain has become, in the telling, another story altogether.

"I guess it's because I used to go up there with Bradley . . . and somehow Bradley and Owen Andersen got mixed up in my mind . . . it was like going back in time, finding a voice where you thought no voice would be. I felt all excited and happy but that was silly."

"Why was it silly?"

"Because Owen couldn't ever be Bradley. And I could never feel that way about anybody else."

"Perhaps you could tell me something more about Bradley," Kovalik says. And I realize, that's who I've been talking about! I never talked to Kovalik about Bradley. How did that happen?

Bradley. A whole world gone to pieces and I can never put them back again, the shape will never be the same. How can I ever explain him properly to Kovalik? You have to sing him, dance him, use music instead of words.

For a few minutes everything is fine. I mean, even though words are inadequate, at least I'm going along, trying to make it clear to Kovalik.

And then the same old thing happens, I get a weird feeling in my throat and I'm terrified that I'm going to cry. I can't bear the thought of crying in that office, the whole thing is too horrible like some soap opera so

I stop talking. Kovalik writes on her pad. I wish I could see what she's writing. It probably says: "Bradley. Who is Bradley? Can't get any more information because patient is all choked up."

"But," I say, and the word pops out and interrupts the soft whispery scratchings of her pencil, "I do feel a lot better. I don't have dreams anymore."

"No dreams at all?"

Maybe she's disappointed to hear it. Or relieved. I wait to see if she'll write again. No more crazy dreams to listen to, thank God. "Oh I have some dreams," I say, "what I mean is I don't wake up in the middle of the night anymore."

No more screams. No more calling Bradley back from nowhere. I guess I've finally accepted the fact that he's not coming back. I can say his name and the wound no longer bleeds. It's just a black-and-blue mark on my heart.

"We'll speak to Dr. Gianni about your medication," Kovalik says, and she writes something down on the pad.

No more pills, this girl is getting sane.

But what is sane? What is getting better? Before it hurt, now it's numb. Will recovery mean forgetting? If that's the case, I'll never recover.

My mother is late picking me up. When she finally drives up, she looks very rushed and nervous. "I have to go over to Grandma's tonight," she says, "she's not feeling well."

"What's wrong with her?"

I dread the thought of my grandmother dying. I hate funerals. I hate all that business about how everyone thinks the dead person looks nice. I had to go to my grandfather's funeral and my mother and grandmother kept saying how they thought he looked "nice and peaceful." They said he looked just like himself again, not the way he looked when he was sick. I thought he looked dead. Not like my grandfather at all. He was like a gray stone, with absolutely nothing left inside.

I didn't have to go to Bradley's funeral. I didn't even know there was one. I was in the hospital, thinking he was alive.

"She works too hard," my mother says. "She wears herself out." My mother is always worrying about my grandmother. She always drives over to do my grandmother's laundry or grocery shopping or ask if she wants her to clean the bathroom and kitchen floors. My grandmother says, "Oh for heaven's sake, Anne, I can take care of myself." It's hard to imagine my mother being a child, a little girl who my grandmother took care of. I wonder what I'll do when my mother gets old. Right now she looks very sad.

"Do you want me to come too?" I ask her.

"No, no," she says, "you have school. I left everything for dinner out on the counter. Put the meat loaf in the oven and set the timer. And make some baked potatoes. Your father will be home early."

She drops me off at the house. Waves good-bye and makes a U-turn and goes back down Ravanna Avenue.

Not until she's gone do I remember that we forgot to have another talk about Owen Andersen.

In the kitchen, the meat loaf is sitting in the baking dish on the counter. There are two potatoes next to it. The table is set with two places. My mother is very efficient.

I stand here staring at the plates on the table and I realize I'm going to be alone with my father. I'm going to have to cook the dinner and serve it and make conversation. That seems like a perfectly normal thing for a daughter to do. The trouble is, I hardly know my father at all.

I put the meat loaf in the oven and set the time. And I keep wondering what we're going to talk about.

THREE

Kovalik is reading my journal:

> Ice-colored glass shadows smashed, yellow flickering silhouettes changing form. Trying to find myself in a hide-and-seek between worlds, catching memories like russet rain petals that float air-green on the changeling in my mind. Forgotten good-byes become hellos.

"I remembered something I forgot," I tell her.

Sitting in the kitchen, reflections in glass from the candles I put on the table. "This is very nice meat loaf, Sandy." Should I tell him I didn't make it? And then a conversation that slides in easy remembering to long unmentioned places. Wait a minute, Dad, have you forgotten who I am? Trodding on fearful ground, the hospital, Sugar Creek, untying the knots of recriminations, helping each other to believe in words again. Until we stop in a heavy, leaden silence. And my father sneezes, breaking the spell, laughing and putting his napkin in front of his face. And suddenly I'm sitting in the waiting room of the Avalands State Hospital, my suitcase is next to my foot. I keep looking down at my white sneakers, asking where they came from, making voice sounds come out of the screeching in my head, words in broken syllables, mismatched nouns and verbs, the babble of disconnected dreams. My mother is on one side of me and somebody else on the other. But wait a minute, it's my father sitting on that side, and all of a sudden gone, as if he'd never been there, gone so quickly that I can't remember his being there at all. And what I haven't remembered in so long is the doorway across the wide room. My father is standing in the doorway, holding something in front of his face. He can't look at his smashed, lame daughter. He turns around.

"We didn't have trouble talking the way I thought we would," I tell Kovalik. "And we made a compromise about Owen Andersen. If I bring him to the house and introduce him and let my parents ask him a lot of questions which I know will be horrible, I can go out with him on Saturday afternoon. We're going to a dog show. I didn't know it but he's very interested in dogs. He knows all kinds of things about breeds and training and showing them. We had a long conversation on the phone, all about dogs, I couldn't believe it. When I told my parents they felt better. It was like he suddenly had an identity. Anybody who knows that much about dogs can't be all bad."

Kovalik smiles but she's not in the mood for jokes. She wants to know more about Bradley. She doesn't exactly force me but she always says the right thing or asks just the right question so she gets me talking. So I tell her more about Deliverance and getting out of there and finally about the accident.

I can feel my throat getting funny. But I keep talking. I have to get it over with. The feeling in my throat spreads to my nose and eyes. It starts crawling around my whole head. I can't wait to get through so I can pull out a tissue and blow my nose. No crying, I keep reminding myself. " . . . so it's better now," I'm saying. "I'm learning to accept the blame."

"Blame," Kovalik asks. "Why?"

Whywhywhywhy like a hot knife slicing through flesh, why picking at the scabs that have grown over and turned to numb stone.

"Because if it hadn't been for me, if *I* hadn't come dragging along, he'd be alive . . . instead of dead."

I can't keep the feeling inside my head any longer, big horrible things start rolling down my cheeks. Tears can't come out of your eyes when you're not crying. But someone's crying. Crying in front of Kovalik, making a big blubbery mess.

"Alexandra, Alexandra," Kovalik's voice says, softly, gently. "Do you need someone to blame? We can't always know the reasons for things happening. We don't always know why."

Even through my slobbery tears I have to smile. Because here's Dr. Kovalik, who's always asking me Why Why Why, saying herself that sometimes there is no answer to that question.

"Bradley's death made you very angry, and very sad. You had to run away from those feelings. You ran away for a long time, Alexandra, do you think you're ready to come back now?"

In the middle of the night I wake up. But not because I'm having a bad dream or I'm feeling frightened or sick again. I go to the closet and fish around in my white prom dress that's hanging in the back. Down through the soft folds of chiffon, my fingers stretch until they touch the newspaper. It's too dark to read the print but I don't have to see to know what it says. A story about Alexandra and Bradley of Ravanna River, who rode in a car driven by Richard Elliott, address unknown. It describes the wreckage as "molten metal, an unrecognizable twisted heap."

"Alexandra Appleton of Ravanna Avenue escaped with serious injuries," it says, and calls it a miracle. Well God, it would have been nice to have two or three miracles instead of only one. Maybe that's why I feel so guilty. What makes me so special?

Instead of putting it back in its hiding place, I tear the newspaper up into a million pieces.

FOUR

In the Trees Again, A New Journal

I was away but now I'm home. I am at the place I left me. I know it's spring but the air is smelling like autumn, a time lost that will come again. All my tears have fallen, have watered seeds which now grow. Sunshine comes through blowy curtains. My heart leaps to be.

Counterpart, you have given me back again. You have made me a person. Living, breathing, walking, talking, a beautiful thing.

Apple Alex Sandy Alexandra, Welcome to the earth.

Outstanding Laurel-Leaf Fiction
for Young Adult Readers

☐ **A LITTLE DEMONSTRATION OF AFFECTION**
Elizabeth Winthrop $1.25
A 15-year-old girl and her older brother find themselves turning
to each other to share their deepest emotions.

☐ **M.C. HIGGINS THE GREAT**
Virginia Hamilton $1.25
Winner of the Newbery Medal, the National Book Award and
the Boston Globe-Horn Book Award, this novel follows M.C.
Higgins' growing awareness that both choice and action lie
within his power.

☐ **PORTRAIT OF JENNIE**
Robert Nathan $1.25
Robert Nathan interweaves touching and profound portraits of
all his characters with one of the most beautiful love stories
ever told.

☐ **THE MEAT IN THE SANDWICH**
Alice Bach $1.25
Mike Lefcourt dreams of being a star athlete, but when hockey
season ends, Mike learns that victory and defeat become
hopelessly mixed up.

☐ **Z FOR ZACHARIAH**
Robert C. O'Brien $1.25
This winner of an Edgar Award from the Mystery Writers of
America portrays a young girl who was the only human being
left alive after nuclear doomsday—or so she thought.

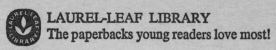

LAUREL-LEAF LIBRARY
The paperbacks young readers love most!

☐ **MAVERICKS** Jack Schaefer
Illustrations by Lorence Bjorklund

"In a magnificent tribute to a vanishing breed of men and horses, the author of *Shane* takes us back to the old Southwest. His mavericks are the invincible mustangs and hard riding cowboys of New Mexico. A superb book."
—*Horn Book* 95¢

☐ **ARE YOU THERE GOD? IT'S ME, MARGARET.**
Judy Blume

Margaret Simon, going on twelve, has a lot to worry about. Making friends in a new school, boys, dances, school projects, growing up physically "normal"—and choosing a religion. $1.25

☐ **CHIEF** Frank Bonham

The gripping struggle of a band of California Indians to survive in the present. 95¢

☐ **FRIEDRICH** Hans Peter Richter

Trapped in Hitler's Nazi Germany, a young Jewish boy struggles to survive. $1.25

☐ **HEY, DUMMY** Kin Platt

A moving story about a young boy's attempt to save a retarded child. $1.25

Buy them at your local bookstore or use this handy coupon for ordering:

Dell | **DELL BOOKS**
P.O. BOX 1000, PINEBROOK, N.J. 07058

Please send me the books I have checked above. I am enclosing $_____
(please add 35¢ per copy to cover postage and handling). Send check or money order—no cash or C.O.D.'s. Please allow up to 8 weeks for shipment.

Mr/Mrs/Miss_____

Address_____

City_____State/Zip_____

"Simply one of the best novels written for any age group this year."—*Newsweek*

I AM THE CHEESE

BY ROBERT CORMIER
AUTHOR OF <u>THE CHOCOLATE WAR</u>

Adam Farmer is a teenager on a suspenseful quest, at once an arduous journey by bicycle to find his father and a desperate investigation into the mysteries of the mind. What exactly is Adam looking for? Where is his father? Why does he have two birth certificates? What is the meaning of his parents' whispered conferences? Of their sudden move to a new town? Of his mother's secret Thursday afternoon phone calls? Of the strange man who appears and reappears in their lives? And why are Adam's thoughts constantly interrupted by an unidentified interrogator who prods him to recall some recent, devastating catastrophe? "The secret, revealed at the end, explodes like an H-bomb."—*Publishers Weekly*

Laurel-Leaf Library $1.50